way to Jenny's death, Coomer tells the moments of their lives with humor and love, creating out of a series of vignettes a rich study of two people in their world.

Interspersed with Mitchell's and Jenny's story is our journey with the storyteller down the dips and turns of the Decatur Road itself—we meet, among others, a river rat, a dog collector, the general store crowd, communists, book-burners, a deadeye rock-thrower, and a mischievous minister—picking up as we go bits and pieces of the mosaic of life in this special place, during this special time. The result is an exceptional novel, a marvelous blend of family saga and social portraiture, the foibles and the sadness and the triumphs of life lived daily, that cannot fail to touch every reader's heart.

THE DECATUR ROAD

THE DECATUR

ROAD JOE COOMER

A Novel of the Appalachian Hill Country

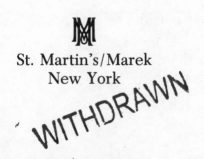

St. Martin's/Marek
New York

Design by Kingsley Parker

Library of Congress Cataloging in Publication Data

Coomer, Joe.
    The Decatur Road.

    I. Title.
PS3553.O574D4 1983   813'.54   83-9610
ISBN 0-312-18998-2

10 9 8 7 6 5 4 3 2

For my family, especially my grandparents,
Joe & Cerilda, and Tom & Frances

ACKNOWLEDGMENTS

First of all, my parents and Karen, and then the members of The Southern Rose and the SMU Literary Festival, and teachers, devoted to literature and students: Laurence Perrine and Ken Shields and Pascal Covici, Jr., and the whole SMU English faculty, and Marsh Terry, whose hug will take all the meanness right out of you, and Bryan Woolley, without whose kindness . . . well, all of you, I am just so grateful.

THE DECATUR ROAD

Most blameless is he, centered in the sphere
Of common duties, decent not to fail
In offices of tenderness . . .

—from Tennyson's "Ulysses"

1

Old tail-wagging weather-beaten dog out in the dry road dust of an August dusk, sparrows strung on barbed wire going hum-flutter, and little puffs of red dirt at the toe of each shoe. There is wind from the east, dry and faint, like the breath of some old woman, but thunder coming after it, coming over his shoulder, coming off the Thacher Knobs: Mitchell Parks walking down the Decatur Road like some proud scarecrow, throwing clods and thinking, well this will make fourteen times that I have done it now and that can only count for the good of me so she will have to give me some answer this time some answer and why shouldn't she say yes most likely she will say yes why not, and chunking a clod at a bird. Mitchell Parks, gangly and stupid-looking unless he concentrates on not looking that way, walking down the Decatur Road westward, flushing birds and petting old dogs, with the late August dust all around him and a September thunder over his shoulder coming on.

"Oh Lord Lord Lord, Momma. I'm gonna do them. Who else does them every night anyway? Lord."

"Young lady, you don't talk to your momma like that."

"Yes, Daddy, but she . . ."

"I said hush."

"Yes, Daddy."

Suds on the worn boards around the basin, no ring on the windowsill, scrubbing hard and furious like resentment.

"Jenny, you're going to rub the special Blue Danube pattern off those dishes. You just slow down or you'll chip a plate."

"Yeeessss, Momma."

"Don't say yes like that to your momma, young lady."

"Yes, Daddy."

Jenny, slight and all elbows, standing at the sink washing Blue Danube, looking out the window down along the Decatur Road with her coal-black belligerent crow eyes, a red rubber band off the Decatur *Advocate-Messenger* holding her hair in a ponytail behind. She thinking well no doubt he is on his way again and will be here before long expecting some answer I suppose some answer so I will have to say something this time and most likely it will be no why shouldn't it be no why not, and banging a dish on the basin rim.

Mitchell Parks is standing there at the side of the house looking through the screen door at Jenny. He has got red road dust on his pants up to his knees, and both of his hands are shoved in his pockets so deep that his shoulders hunch forward. He is thinking, Jesus would you look at her hair all tied up with that rubber band why don't she take that off so her hair will go on her shoulders why don't she do that.

Jenny is standing there too, holding the knob of the screen door tight with both hands. It is getting dark now and heavy summer thunder echoes over the Decatur Road, the dry fields, the house. There is a bare yellow bulb above the screen door with the remnant of a swallow nest clinging to it. The bulb is burning and a big gray, dust-covered moth flutters toward and away. The first drop of rain falls on the dirt yard.

Mitchell says this: "Doesn't your hair hurt where it is all bunched up together with that rubber band? I bet you couldn't get one more hair inside that rubber band."

"No," she says back, and then she adds this: "And don't you talk about my hair anyway."

So Mitchell shoves his hands farther down in his pockets and it scares Jenny so that she whispers real fast and hard, "Don't pull your pants down here, God! Daddy will kill you."

"I wasn't going to."

"For God's sake let me be, Mitchell Parks. You have come now and said the things you have said. So just go."

"I will open that door there you are holding and kiss you."

"You will not."

"But it was you who kissed me first."

"I said no."

"But I have a right to know. I have done my part in the asking. I have come all this way."

"I can't decide now. I will decide later. The next time you come."

"No. I have come all this way. It is starting to rain. You tell me."

"All right then, all right. I will just say No then. And that will serve you."

"I will kiss you, I will."

"You will not, Mitchell Parks. If I open the door flies will get in the house, and I have spent all day killing them."

"It is raining harder now, Jenny."

"I know it is, Mitchell."

"I will come and open that door there."

"No." He thinks I will say yes because of the rain on his hat. He thinks I will marry him for the rain. "You go on home, Mitchell Parks. You scare me sometimes. Go on home."

"I will just stand here in the rain forever. I will just wait forever."

"You don't want me."

3

"I want you."

"The rain is setting in steady, Mitchell. Go on home. Go on away from here before I cry."

"No."

"Go on, I said."

"No, I deserve some chance. Give me some chance. I want you."

"I will call my daddy, I will, and then you will go."

"I won't."

So Jenny turns and yells this: "Daddy, Mitchell Parks won't go on and walk home in the rain."

And from within the house: "Well, invite him in, sugar."

And Mitchell Parks says, "Your daddy likes me."

And she turns back, her black eyes taking wing. "I suppose you think I will have to marry you now, don't you, Mitchell Parks, don't you."

And Mitchell Parks, gangly and stupid-looking unless he concentrates on not looking that way, concentrates, and slowly says, "If you open the door real quick, maybe no flies will get in."

Thunder break across the valley and wind, hard now, and rain, rain on the dry spot where Mitchell Parks stood, and out in the Decatur Road an old wet tail-dragging dog.

2

If you have no horse, much less an automobile, it is a long walk from the outskirts of the county into Decatur. You can cut two miles off the Decatur Road by walking through a few acres of tobacco and hay and crossing the Muskatatuck, but you take your chances. There may be dogs you don't know or the river may be up too deep to wade. Worse, you may run into John Alford, who lives down on the river bottom, and get into a conversation. But these are the bad things. If you are half-lucky there will be no strange dogs, and somebody will have thrown some crossing rocks in the Muskatatuck since the last rain, and John Alford won't see you until you're across the river, and you can pretend you don't hear old Alford yelling. Then it is just a short step back to the road again, and there you are with the extra two miles in your pocket.

But you are taking the shortcut ahead of its time. There is eight miles of walking on the Decatur Road before you even have the option of saving the two miles. You are way ahead of yourself.

It just comes out of nowhere. There is the western slope of the Appalachians, and then the Thacher Knobs, and then there is the Decatur Road coming out of the forest. It is hard to tell whether the trees are starting to grow in the middle of the road or the road is just marching its way deeper into the mountains. From where the road starts to the center of Decatur is about thirty-two miles. If you say it is thirty-one or thirty-three or thirty-two miles exactly, you will have an argument on your hands because no one agrees where the road actually starts. One person will tell you it starts just a bit beyond Tom Webster's house and the next will say the road opens up a mile and a half farther on, where the Quirks Run breaks from the Thacher Knobs, where old man Parks keeps his goats. At the Perry's Landing Store on the Muskatatuck you will hear a big argument about all of this five or six times a year. It always ends when Johnson Daniels, the mediator in all things, says, "Well, it either starts at Webster's, or it starts at Parks', one or the other." And this seems to satisfy everyone for a month or two: "Yeah, yeah, that's true." "One or the other." "You always hit it on the head,

Johnson Daniels." And then Johnson Daniels nods and puts his pipe back in his mouth.

But you are ahead of yourself again. Perry's Landing Store is nine miles down the Decatur Road from Parks'. You are excited and trying to tell this story too fast. You must say the simple, large things first.

3

"But what is wrong with this bed? We have slept on it for seven nights now."

"There is nothing wrong with it. It is a good bed, a fine bed, but it is not our bed. It is your bed. I want one that will be ours."

"But we don't even have a house to put it in," said Mitchell Parks, exasperated.

"When we have a house, the bed will be ours to put in it. The first thing. I won't sleep another night on this bed."

"Then you will have to sleep on the floor for a while. It will take days to make a good frame, not to mention the flocks of birds to be feathered."

"I will sleep on the floor."

"We will argue our whole lives long."

"That will make them worthwhile," said Jenny Parks.

Mitchell walked around the room for a few minutes. Then he walked over to the window and looked out. Finally her smile in the small of his back became unbearable and he said, "I guess you can take that part about sleeping on the floor back if you want to."

In the early winter, after the first snowfall, evenings in the Thacher Knobs begin at four o'clock. When the sun gets within a foot of the horizon it turns kingfisher and dives as if this dive were the last of the season. The coldness then comes very hard and fast, and with it a stillness. But it is a cold you can take, in the early winter, a cold that you dare by going out to the barn in your undershirt to get more firewood. And the stillness, that is something that you can only look at and think about. The whole early winter is like a summer pre-storm stillness. The trees stand at an angle to the knobs, and looking up at them, more than anything else you would call them quiet. To see a bird come over the ridge and fly, faintly, across the gap, is something almost miraculous. And the snowfall itself, falling, drifting in with the half-light, simply closes down the outside.

The new fire in the stove warmed the room just enough to make the quilts on the new bed inviting. But she would wait for him. She wondered what was taking him so long —the room was getting warmer quickly, and she wanted them to go to bed while it was still cold. She sat on the edge of the bed, bringing her knees up so she could fold her arms around them. She shuddered, and tucked the white cotton hem of her nightgown under her feet. And already, this soon, she was remembering the first night, when he said to her, "Hurry up, I warmed up your side for you," and she thought it such a wonderful thing for someone to say to her that it made her shy, shier than she promised herself she would be, and she stood across the bedroom, staring down and smiling at the button on her nightgown for a full silent minute before she went to him. It was already good to remember it.

And this was the new bed. Their bed. Heavy oak with a poplar railing along the head and footboard, and along the top of the headboard holes were bored, evenly spaced, waiting for hand-carved pegs. A peg for each child. She squirmed and bounced on the bed to make the fittings and joints squeak. They were good smooth groans,

7

not sharp pops. And she had a thought, and she thought it was a wonderful thought, that these squeaks would be with her all her life, and losing all control, she unclasped her arms and clapped. The claps bounced around the small room, she waiting and listening for them, until the deep feather mattress drew each clap in and made the room quiet again.

It had been too late in the year to pull the feathers off Mr. Parks' geese, and so she had gone to her mother for help. Together they made the rounds to each aunt and niece and grandmother, collecting small bags of unused feathers and old pillows, until they had gathered almost seventeen pounds of duck and goose down. The whole bed had cost them $1.26, and that for the heavy blue-and-white ticking used to hold and shape the feathers into a somewhat oval lumpy rectangle. It was her touch, the four heavy seams down the center length of the mattress. She told her mother it was for strength and to help hold the shape. Her mother said she had never seen anyone else do it that way and that it would simply make the mattress sag in the middle. She had done all of this, insisted on the bed, insisted on the seams, seven days after the wedding. It would take, she had thought, seven days to know. And she felt she knew. She had sat on the corner of the old bed, much as this night, and thought he is a good man, I could have fallen in love with a man who was not good, but I have fallen in love and I have fallen in love with a good man. I guess I am lucky. I will have him make the bed now.

And the four seams, the four extra tucks—so that nine times out of ten in the night, if he wasn't thinking about it, he would roll to the center, and she would be there already, waiting for him.

The room was warm now, and the light from the stove and the two small bedlamps seemed to varnish the walls and furniture, the bricks of the old fireplace. Jenny put

8

her feet on the still cold floor and pushed herself up from the bed. She saw her reflection in one of the four panes of the one window and went to touch it. It was cold, and as soon as she put her finger to it she lost herself to the outside. The light from the room shone faintly on the snow beneath the window and she could only barely make out her silhouette and the shadows of the window's crosspieces on the whiteness. She leaned to the right and put her face close to the glass trying to see if Mitchell was still in the barn, but the angle was wrong. The snow fell lightly across the hollow. She tried to catch sight of single flakes as soon as they came into the faint light thrown from the room and follow them down until they rested with the others. A large one surprised her as it was swept up by the wind and swerved directly at her. She had focused in on it and as it came toward her she had to cross her eyes. It finally made her duck and it made her giggle after it.

It was darker here. That was one difference. In Decatur there were lights burning all night, and from a mile out you could see a foggy glow over the town. And it was quieter here. The animals made a racket in the morning, but if you woke up, there was something to wake up to. She and her parents drove up two weeks before the wedding to look at Mr. Parks and Mitchell's place. It was an old house, large on the outside and small inside: the walls were five layers thick: log, two sets of weatherboard, shingles, and cedar paneling inside. It was a tight house, and Jenny's father liked it. The house sat in the farthest reach of a hollow and was surrounded by barns, shacks, wellhouses, and great round-topped maples. And there were goats everywhere, eating everything, smelling and nipping at Jenny's mother, until she got back in the Ford and sat there. There had been no women for her to talk to, and she felt left out and left alone, and she cried on the trip home.

Mitchell, his father, and two brothers worked the farm. The goats and the tobacco allotment paid for everything, with enough to put Mitchell's younger brother Brice through the state school in Lexington. Mitchell and his older brother Stilman fixed up Mitchell's room so Jenny and he would be comfortable until they got their house built.

She sat back down on the bed and wondered what his mother had been like. The picture of her on the bureau was brown and had a spot on it, but she was still beautiful. The photographer had added a touch of blue to her eyes and a pink shading to her cheeks. It must have been her bureau. And looking at the picture reminded her of her own mother and the fourteenth time that Mitchell came down the Decatur Road: He was sitting inside with her mother and father talking while she pouted in the kitchen and looked at the rain. And all of the sudden she heard her mother say that country people were just different from city people and that was all there was to it. And it struck her deeply somehow that Mitchell was in there alone and must be hurting without her. Then she heard him stutter and finally speak, and there and then, in the kitchen alone, she decided to say yes when he said, "People in the city aren't much different; they know about more things, because there's more people to make things happen. But they aren't much different than country; they don't know any more about love or hate or God or death; a man alone knows as much about those things as a whole city." She thought it was such a pitiful sorry thing for anyone to say, and it made her sorry for him, especially when she heard her mother laugh. And then her father said, "Those are good thoughts, Mitchell," and she almost cried for being sorry for him. And the wonderful thing was that Mitchell didn't feel sorry for himself.

She had waited too long to tell him that evening. The rain stopped and he started home. He was all the way to

10

the crest of the hill when she stepped out of the screen door into the yard. He was walking over the hill and all she could see were his shoulders and head when she cupped her hands to her mouth. When she screamed at the top of her lungs the words, "Well, all right then, Mitchell Parks," he had completely disappeared. But the night had darkened around her by now, and in the darkness she could make out a shape coming at her and it was a bouncing shape, and at first she thought it was some wild jumping goat, but then the sound of it got to her and it was a human sound, and it was Mitchell Parks, running back down the hill toward her house at top speed, yelling, she thought, like a drunk out of his mind. And it scared her so much that she jumped back inside the house and held the screen door tight again and cried and cried as Mitchell skidded down into her yard and fell and slid fourteen feet in the mud and then got up and jumped down in it again for good effect, jumping and rolling in the mud through the night and into the morning.

And this made her remember the second night, when she got up the nerve to tell him that his feet were cold and big, and they talked about themselves and the future, and, in short, they were serious. The night had lingered on, and they were both deeply melancholy about their love, and about the mystery of it and the world around them, and she had said something she had seen at a movie that was perfect for the time, "Well, we won't say anything about sadness or happiness for right now. For right now we will just say that there will be the two of us. Okay?" And Mitchell had not answered, he had just lain there for a few moments, and then he had said, very softly, so softly that it almost sounded earnest, that he was sorry he had big cold feet. And so she dug her elbows, which were like needles, into his ribs.

All of these things came to her there in the night. And they made her think of herself and how young she was and how old the world was and how much she wanted to be a poet in it. It wasn't the word she thought, but it was the word she meant. And she thought that thinking about being a poet automatically shut off her chances because a poet was a poet, and did not think about being one. But suddenly, as she was thinking, sitting there on the edge of her bed in her nightgown, a man in an undershirt stuck his head in the door to her bedroom, and it frightened her so that she jumped on the other side of the bed and screamed. And then she recognized Mitchell and said, "Oh." It was an easy thing to do, two weeks after your wedding, to be alone in a room, sitting on the edge of the bed, thinking about things like you always have, and completely forget that you were married.

He brought in an armful of snow-flaked firewood, and from behind his back he produced a pine branch with a few withered cones, the whole sparkling with a thin layer of ice. And he gave it to her. And she looked at it and she looked at him. He built a fire in the old fireplace, hardly used since the stove was put in, and she put the green branch on the hearth, and they went to bed. And in the night the ice on the branch melted, and the needles steamed and wilted and then began to smoke. And as they slept, and the house slept, and the snow fell, the green bough rose and flamed, burned bright and blue, and died away. There on the hearth, in the middle of the night.

4

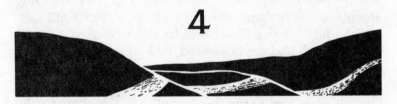

So out of the mountains it comes, down out of the Thacher Knobs alongside the Quirks Run, playing tag with the creek, crossing over and through it where the slate is flat and solid under the water: the Decatur Road. And it comes subtly at first, the road, choosing the same path that a rock might, falling down the knobside; so subtly it comes that you are walking along it before you have noticed, walking along what would be a leaf-covered animal path in the summer but what is now a meandering whiter line of snow stretching through the bramble-marred whiteness of the forest floor. And this whiter line falls and turns out of the mountains until it runs into a huge other whiteness, a sycamore six feet around bending up out of the snow and losing itself in the whiteness of the sky. But on the other side of the tree, opposite the path, breaks a two-rut road so suddenly that you would swear some eons ago some fellow had come walking down the path with his stick and had stopped to rest there for a while and had decided he was so sick of walking that then and there he invented the wheel and axle.

And so you go on walking, having come down out of the mountains and forest alone like the rock and the path to the two-rut road, and you realize that someone, at least one person with a cart or a wagon or a car, has come this far, has been here before, and has simply missed you. Then you have a glimpse of that other great phenomenon, the one other than solitude, and it puts the fear and excitement of an adventure into you. So you walk faster. But the Decatur Road is still quiet here, goes along without making a sound unless it makes one of its crossings over the Quirks Run to smoother, easier going. The creek is new and you can jump it with a five- or six-step start, and that is a good thing when the water is ice-clogged and cold. And at any moment, it seems, the two ruts of the road could go around a bend and run into a giant sycamore. It seems the road could end that easily. The branches of the nearby trees, ice- and snow-laden, lean out over the road, crowding it out as if it had no right to be there. Oak and poplar and pine seedlings line the snowy mound between the two ruts as if they were on some God-bidden odyssey into the interior. And even knowing that it would be senseless, the road ending out here in the forest, you still have the feeling that it may, that it might, and you wonder what you would do then.

But as you wonder, the road drops out of a niche between two knobs into a hollow one hundred yards wide, and stretches itself alongside the creek down the middle of the small valley. There is tobacco stubble, thick-stemmed and sharp but still sprouting green this midwinter, alongside the road at this first flat acre out of the mountains, and at the head of the hollow the road leaves the creek, roams in and out of a group of shacks and barns and goat pens, and then fairly widens and prostrates itself in the front yard of an old log house. Then there is another niche between two knobs and the Decatur Road catches up to the Quirks Run, and together they go on running, tight and narrow and fast.

5

"It's a terrible thing to happen, marring their expected happiness," said Mrs. Bridwell, and she continued her mount up the hillside, holding the skirt of her dress up from the frozen mud and dirty snow. Her husband shook his head and followed her, his hands clasped behind his back.

They were all standing there, all who knew him, except those who were too sick or too old to make it up the hill. Mitchell and his two brothers stood side by side, their hats in their hands, talking to Pastor Lawson. At odd moments men would come up and shake the brothers' hands and then turn and walk away. It was cold. The sky was light gray but the wind pushed smaller, darker clouds swiftly underneath the overcast. The children marched around the cemetery in a tight dark bunch, reading the inscriptions to each other. It had snowed during the night, and each tombstone had an even white cap of powder along the top and the epitaphs and engraved roses and angels all had white borders. Mitchell Parks looked up from his hands and said, "Well, all right, let's get started. It's cold out here."

And so Pastor Lawson stepped to the head of the open grave and waited patiently for the groups of people to notice him and walk silently toward him. There were six wooden folding chairs set out for the three brothers and their father's brother and sister, and Jenny. Mitchell remembered his wife and helped her sit in a chair, and then he helped the old aunt sit, too.

The old aunt sat still for a few moments, and then, since she had never spoken to Jenny other than at their meeting, put her old brown hand on Jenny's knee and said, "How far along are you, honey?"

"Eight months, ma'am."

"It's a sad time, isn't it?"

Mitchell and his brothers stood at the side of the grave, but the uncle, who had come and looked down into the grave once, stayed away from the group, stayed off and looked away.

And so they stood there, all who were able that knew him, and listened. "The best proof of heaven is that some people deserve . . ." But, the wind, it got in the way for Mitchell Parks, and at first he tried to break through it and hear the words, but it was too much for him. So he thought about the wind, thought about the wind the way you might watch a ripple in a stream for hours one day and

15

then forget it for the rest of your life, as if that time had never existed but for the breathing through it.

The morning after it happened, in the early morning after it happened, he was out in the barn working. He was working on the gearbox of the mowing machine. It was broken. There must have been a broken gear; maybe a gear with a broken tooth. This was what was needed to be done: There were the four bolts of the plate steel outer covering to be removed and then you could get to the works: easy done. There were the clamps holding the shafts in solidly: two clamps, four bolts: yes. The spring steel C-clips and the bearings: worn but okay. And then the gears, the gears in succession, in sequence, one after another, and here, yes, here it was, the broken tooth, jammed in a free-wheeling sister gear; and as he worked he saw a hand reaching into the works, working at the broken part, not his hand, although this hand was attached to his forearm, not his hand, which was sinewy and taut, but a hand that was tanned, strong, meaty and calloused, a hand that had reached down before him and fixed the broken parts before, a hand he knew: his father's hand. He pulled it back.

And the days between the death and the burial were like this for him. They were a counting off, a rote list of action repeatedly broken by images that frightened and angered him, reminded him. He would count the strokes of his wood-chopping and his father would tell him to be careful; he would ignore this, counting faster, closer, counting his own breathing till he would grow weak and nauseous with his sweat in the winter and would sit down and think the words as clearly as he could think them, thinking the words on purpose, up front, in order to burn them off, to rid himself of them: So this is how it is. This is how it was to be. I was to find this woman, to love this woman, and she was to love me. And we were to be allowed to be together and to know each other and to be happy. So that we would expect happiness, know it to be in front of us and for us. So that I would come to believe that the child was free, cost only love and caring and work. This is how it was to be and this is how it has come to pass. Rising each morning expecting the child, expecting my fatherhood, but rising finding my father, losing my father.

But not crying over this. His father had lasted through the night, had lasted through the blue cold and the winds and the falling snow, lasted until he could see the opening of the shuttered windows and watch the sun rise like some stark flabbergasted angel through the clouds, rise like Jesus, his old father had said. And his old father had said that this wasn't a sad time, had said that he was going to join his wife. Had, in fact, waited for this day for nineteen years, had seen the years through, had done his love and duty toward his boys. "You are all able now, boys," he had said. And the old man had faded before them and the room had faded, the furniture blending into the walls before their eyes, so that they could not focus as they left the room and they ran into things.

Not crying over the lost father, not crying over his loss. The service had ended, and Mitchell carried his wife back down the hill to a neighbor's wagon, told her she weighed a ton, and said he would be home soon. He and his brothers put their father in the ground and covered him over. The clods of earth were frozen, but they smoothed the mound as much as they could, and then gathered pine boughs and laid them on the grave. They put their coats back on, and picked up their shovels and stood there, not knowing how to leave. And then Stilman, the only one of them who could really remember their mother, took one of the frozen boughs and laid it on the grave next to their father's. They walked home, three miles back up the Decatur Road.

There were two hours of daylight left after they had gotten home and eaten supper. Brice began packing his clothes for the trip back to school. Mitchell and Stilman both got up from the table and went for the ax by the back door. Mitchell stopped short and looked at his brother.

Stilman said, "You go on; I used it yesterday."

"No, I think I'd rather go out and curry Barney. We've sort of left him off the past couple days."

"Well." And Stilman put the ax over his shoulder and went to the wood lot.

Mitchell stepped out the door after him and almost shut it on Jenny. She stepped out into the twilight, onto the crusting snow, and said, "I'm going out to the barn with you." So he put his arm around her waist and helped her step along. It was warmer in the barn. Hay was stacked along both of the side walls and in the loft overhead. A dry, loose dirt floor ran the length of the place, and along the left-hand side, hidden by the bales of hay, were stalls for two beef cattle, a Jersey, and the old mule, Barney. Mitchell built a throne of hay bales for Jenny, lined it with a wool blanket, put her in it, and then, after wrapping the blanket around her, broke open a bale and covered her up to the chin with the loose hay. Then he stepped into a recess in the stacked hay and came out a minute later followed by a slab-flanked sixteen-hand mule chewing on a corncob. Mitchell set a bucket of grain on the ground and let the mule eat while he combed out the matted hair. It was quiet. The Jersey had murmured when they came in, but the hay seemed to muffle the outside and warm up the inside so much that it made them sleepy. Jenny sat still and watched. Mitchell kept combing the mule. Once he said, "Ol' Barney," and patted him on the flank. And he combed until he was finished, while Jenny watched, then gave the mule another cob to chew on and put him up. He lifted Jenny out of the hay, and they walked back to the house through the snow and the night.

Mitchell built a fire in the bedroom stove just before they went to bed. Together they watched it die, and still he did not say anything, simply lay there, holding Jenny close to him. And she was crying in her throat long before Mitchell knew she was crying, and it was a silent crying, a crying she laid upon his chest and let him feel. And it was all he needed. He let her head rest under his chin, and he smelled of her hair and pressed against it with his lips and cheek. And he cried, cried silently, and tears came out of the one eye closest to the pillow and he had to open his mouth to help him breathe. Crying over this: not crying over his loss, the death, but crying for the time his father had spent without his wife, crying for his last nineteen years alone. And it wore him out, the crying and the holding back, and he fell asleep with it, and she fell asleep next to him.

It was later, later in the night, when the fire was long out but still would have shown red coals if you'd poked it with a stick, that he woke up. It puzzled him, because he did not know what had awakened him, and he listened to the outside closely, held his breath to help him listen. And then it happened: A foot, it was unmistakably a foot, struck swiftly through Jenny's stomach and kicked him hard below his last rib in the solar plexus, and it caught him so off guard, a complete surprise, that he said something like "uuuaann," and fell off the bed; in the moment of falling, frightened out of his mind, and knowing what had happened and then laughing as he struck the hardwood floor. And he lay there on the floor in the middle of the night laughing out loud till Jenny, eyes half closed, put her head out over the edge of the bed and looked at him, and looked at him again, and fell back asleep and woke up, and he was still laughing, his abdomen silently rising and falling in the quiet of the night.

She had labored through the night, had labored through a long, cold mid-February starlit night, labored until she could see the moon drop over the ridge like someone who had waited as long as he could and now had to leave or he would be late for some other appointment. And every five minutes either the old aunt or Mrs. Bridwell would come out to Mitchell in the kitchen and say, "She is a-ticking like a clock now, Mitchell Parks, and it will not be so long now." And Mitchell Parks would get up off the kitchen table with a big red mark on his cheek where he had rested his palm and punch one of his brothers or his uncle in the shoulder. And then the old aunt came out once more and Mitchell got ready to punch a shoulder and both of his brothers gave a feint and showed their fists back at him, and then they all noticed that the aunt was carrying this little baby. Mitchell peeked over the blanket it was wrapped in and said softly, "Look at it." And then louder, "Look here, Stilman, would you just look here, Brice." And he took the baby in his arms and asked about Jenny and smiled and said he was going in to see her when Mrs. Bridwell backed out of the bedroom door with a bawling baby.

Stilman said, "Another one. A pair."

Brice said, "Gawd."

The old aunt, empty-handed, whispered in the uncle's ear, "Bridwell's always trying to upstage me."

And Mitchell Parks rose up on tiptoes and thought, Well, this is something new to think about. And his face got all slack and stupid-looking because he wasn't concentrating.

And after all the excitement of the morning, Mitchell went into the bedroom and looked at his wife and son and daughter and he thought of a funny thing to say to make

20

Jenny laugh and so he said it. He said, "I want to know which one of you young'un's been kicking me off the bed." And it was such a funny thing that he said, that he laughed at his own joke, lay down on the floor with laughing at his own joke.

The morning after it happened, he was out in the barn working on a second crib, replacing slats and sanding old paint off the headboard. And it occurred to him that he had never seen his father do this, and he had the thought that he still did not understand, would probably never understand, and it slowed his sanding for a moment as he thought. He finished the sanding, though, put the crib up on a bale of hay to give it a good look, and suddenly said out loud, "I love you, old Pop." And afraid that he might laugh or cry out there alone in the barn, he grabbed the crib, pulled his coat tight around him, and made a dash across the barn lot to the house.

He stands on the hill and watches Mitchell Parks come down the trail toward him. Well, what is he throwing up and down I wonder, wonders crazy old man Alford, and he crouches behind a thick stand of young fir. Mitchell walks past and John Alford, lean as an old cat and slack all over, jumps out of the trees and grabs Mitchell's arm and out of nowhere starts a conversation. Oh my gosh, thinks Mitchell Parks.

"Well, what are you up to, Parks-boy?"

"Going to Decatur, Mr. Alford."

"I've been to Decatur every year of my life, son. What you got in your hand?"

"Mowin'-machine gear. Broke it last fall. Gonna need it this spring."

"Well, you're damn right you're gonna need it. Black your eye, boy, you're gonna need it."

"Yep."

"I didn't make it to your daddy's funeral. But he was a

good man; he used to talk to me every time he took the shortcut, didn't try to cut and hide like some."

"He was a good man."

"Dunk your face in a pond, he was a good man. Your wife bear out yet?"

"Yep. Come up with two, a boy and a girl."

"Break your foot, a boy and a girl."

"Yep," said Mitchell Parks, "one and an extra." And he smiled and patted old John Alford on the back as he left him, skidding across the ice of the Muskatatuck on his way back to the Decatur Road.

Old John Alford, he mounted back up the knobside, shaking his head every once in a while, till he reached the top and looked back down on the river, and at Mitchell Parks, mounting the opposite knobside. And he shook his head again, and he, that old man, that crazy old fool, as if he understood, up there alone on the knob above the slow-moving Muskatatuck, he winked, and shook his head, and said, "Stump your toe."

6

Tight and narrow and fast down through the Thacher Knobs go the Decatur Road and the Quirks Run, and then tight, narrow, and slow goes the Decatur Road back up them: nine miles of knobs to the Muskatatuck and rolling hills. It is leg-breaking work, this knob-walking; it is all up- or downhill, and you find that the tendons in your ankles have had a good stretching when you are through walking. Knobs are the carbuncles of this earth. They are steep: things are continually rolling off of them and trees send out roots that grab on to anything available. And they are crowded, seemingly having forced their way up between one another's shoulders and armpits as if there were some spectacle to be seen in the sky. It is best to follow a creek down between them, since the water has had all eons of time to find the easiest way. But even the water has a hard time of it, having to make a hundred-foot leap downward at times, and every once in a while a creek will run up against a knob so obstinate that the water has to make a lake of itself just to get a thin trickle over the top. There are two creeks, strong running, with lots of momentum, that you would think would run to the ends of the earth, which simply drop into a hole in a knob and are never seen again. Yes, these knobs are strange business when it comes to getting out of them, and it will wear you out just to think about them. The Quirks Run seems to make its way fairly well, though, and so the Decatur Road goes along with it as much as possible, only separating from the creek when there is some interesting landmark close by or a good view is to be had.

Still it is no more than a two-rut road after it leaves the Parks place, a two-rut road running alongside a shallow knob ditch for almost a mile and a half until it reaches Tom Webster's farm. Here the mound of grass gradually disappears from the center of the road, and two small tributaries join the Quirks Run making it into a respectable stream. Here also is the first bridge of the Decatur Road crossing over the creek; before this point the road just picking a likely spot and wading right through. This is where the big argument comes in, the one that Johnson Daniels always mediates: There are no houses in between the Parks and Webster places. The Decatur Road, down to Webster's, isn't much more than a thought of a foothold because the Parkses are the only people who use it, and they've only got one spindly hay wagon and one slab-flanked mule that they don't even ride because he's too old. Half the county says that the Decatur Road from

Parks' to Webster's is no more than a glorified driveway to Parks' goat farm, and therefore isn't rightfully the Decatur Road. This seems to settle everything until somebody remembers that he walked up that road once to fish in a pond, or look for ginseng, or to hunt, and if it was somebody's driveway that would have been trespassing. It is then that Johnson Daniels takes his pipe from his mouth and mediates. It is a tedious argument, dating back to 1922, when the county proposed a plan to gravel all official county roads. Old Tom Parks wanted gravel on his road. The county estimated that getting gravel over that particular mile and a half would have cost about six times as much as any other mile and a half, estimated that the only feasible alternative was to put a thinner layer of gravel from Perry's Landing up to Parks'. Well, that brought an uproar, with everybody from Perry's to Webster's on the Decatur Road who wasn't a special friend of Tom Parks saying that he didn't want no thin-graveled half-ass road, saying that Parks could just go without gravel, had all these years. But all of this came to nothing. A year after the county proposal, the deputy mayor put an article in the Decatur *Advocate-Messenger* saying that there wasn't any money after all, that the Decatur Road debate was likely never to end, that the proposal was only a proposal anyway. Not one person between the Perry's Landing Store and the Parks place has seen a gravel laying in the Decatur Road to this day.

Tom Webster has a new bridge in down here where the Decatur Road shoots off to the Parks place (and it is not that much of a bridge to be proud of, three logs and eight rough planks). Tom's great endeavoring is perspective. He lives on one of the highest knobs in the area so that he may get out and "look around him." "The world is thrown over by perspective. It all has to do with angles and light and shadow." He will meet someone and will bob and contort his upper torso to the point of dizziness gathering details about the person's face from different

24

perspectives. His wife is ugly from every angle but one, and he will tell you himself that if he is not careful he may not see her from the correct perspective all day long. He is always happy to tell you if you are seeing something from the wrong viewpoint . . . will give you a few hints . . . will tell you that perspective will someday overthrow this earth. This is what he told old Tom Parks about his way of seeing the gravel situation, said old Tom just needed to bend a little lower or stand up on tiptoes to see things right. Old Tom Parks, oh, he was a live one, everyone says. He went home that night, dammed up the Quirks Run in a hollow, and then let it go the next morning. Tom Webster's little bridge made a fine raft, floated all the way to the Muskatatuck eventually. Some boys used it to fish off one whole summer. Tom Webster, all he could do was screw up his mouth and say, "Perspective."

7

In the winter you cannot go outside and pick an onion out of the ground and eat it. So you dig coal.

Jan. 6

My Darling Jenny,

It sure feels funny having to write a letter to you. I don't think I like it. Since you've gotten this letter, I guess you know that we've made it all right. It was a longer trip than we thought because the mine is six miles outside of Jackson. Stilman said to tell you hello and to spank Becky and Henry for him. Give them a kiss for me. I love you.

Mitchell

Mitchell Parks,

I am so mad at you that I would scream if I thought you could hear it. That was the most pitiful letter I have ever gotten in my life, and to think that my own husband wrote it. You listen to me, don't bother to lick the envelope if you don't fill up two pages and take the total worth of the stamp. I want to know where you're living, what you're doing, and who's feeding you. I hope this is understood. Tell Stilman I said hello.

Jennifer

Jan. 15

My Darling Jenny,

I am sorry. The first week Stilman and I didn't do much but hang around and stand in line. There are hundreds of men here all looking for work. If we had gotten here any later I don't think they would have taken us. Me and Stilman and two other men, Steven Beggs and Aaron Courtright, share a big white tent. There are about seventy or eighty other tents just like ours. The camp can get pretty messy with all the tramping around. But when it snows it's real pretty. The food isn't the best, and the lines are long to get it. Stilman is going to see if he can't change his job and be a cook. His cooking would sure do the camp a lot better. There are a couple things that we had to get mad at, but it doesn't seem like we can do much. They wouldn't let me and Stilman work together. Since he's so much shorter than me, he has to work in the very bottom of the mine where they are digging new shafts. It takes him an hour to get to the bottom and an hour and a half to get back to the top, and he don't even get paid for that time. I work in what they call the cavern. It's a big shaft where me and seven other men put up beams to hold the roof up. The very first day we were here two men got hurt because there wasn't enough support in the shaft. My job is a lot safer than most. The hardest thing about it is getting clean afterward, especially since we don't have any hot water. They don't allow us to make fires because somebody's always burning a tent down. I need to tell you right now that I miss you and love you so much. I wish to God I was home. Another thing we didn't like was the way they pay us. They don't give us money. They give us these tokens that we use for money in their company store. Everything seems awful high in the store too. That means Stilman and me are going to have to carry everything when we come home next month. We've rounded up a couple of bean sacks but that won't carry it all. I don't know what we're going to do. I got to go now. I hope I've written enough. Tell my babies I love them. I love you.

Mitchell

Jan. 21

Dear Mitchell,

I am sorry I got mad and yelled at you. I miss you and love you too. Becky and Henry miss you too, I can tell. Everything you tell me sounds perfectly horrible. I think you must have the most dangerous job or you wouldn't have said it was the safest. I think you and Stilman ought to just leave the tent to the others and come on home. We could make it without you both having to be from home and chancing getting killed. I don't like it. Your brother Brice has been coming home from school every weekend to see if me and the kids are all right even though you and I both told him he didn't have to. He has a friend that drives home to Decatur every weekend and he gets a lift with him. You write him a letter and tell him to stop it, I know he has got to study. Don't worry about anything here. Becky had a cold for a couple days but is fine now. Henry is being his usual self and getting into everything.

I took him out to the barn with me yesterday to milk the cow and you ought to have seen the things I had to slap out of his hand before he put them in his mouth. I am only getting five or six eggs a day now. It's just too cold for the hens. I am making you and Stilman extra warm shirts for when you come home. I miss you and be careful.

Love, Jenny

P.S. The billy goat got mad at having to stay outside in the cold and busted his head through to the inside of the barn but couldn't get anything else in after it. Then I guess he found out he couldn't pull his head back out either. So he has been that way for two days now, stuck in the barn, halfway in and halfway out. I walked in the barn and thought somebody had killed him and mounted his poor head on the wall. Every night I go in the barn and feed his head and then go outside and put blankets on his backside. It is a lot of walking to take care of one animal. But he should only have to stay that way for a few more days till Brice gets here and can get him out. I'm not strong enough, and besides that, I can't decide which end of him scares me the most. ha ha.

Love, Jenny

Jan. 26

My Darling Wife,

You sure can put a lot of things in one letter. I do not have the most dangerous job. I am more worried about the billy goat than I am about myself. But I guess Brice will have taken care of him by the time you get this. Jenny, there are so many fellas here that are worse off than we are. They got no homes to go to or nobody to call theirs. We are lucky. Stilman got the cooking job and really likes it. It made him friends with everybody at the mine and he brings home (the tent) leftovers to me and Steve and Aaron. He said that all those years he cooked for us after Mom died did him some good. He is a lot happier here than I am. It is like he has a bunch of little brothers to take care of again. All of the men call him Mom and Pop because he takes care of the sick fellas in camp and gives advice on everything. He is really much happier here than he is at home, especially since Daddy died, and is talking about staying on past March. I told him we needed him at home. He said that he had always felt funny since you came, because you did most of the things he used to. I told him I was sorry, but he said it was supposed to be that way, and that he wouldn't trade you or the kids for anything. I still hope he comes home with me in March. I would miss him awful. He talked for almost ten minutes about staying. I've never seen him talk that long about anything. We have figured out this month's trip home anyway. A man who's going through Decatur on his way to Hopkinsville is going to give us and the food a lift in his wagon for a sack of potatoes. We thought it was a fair deal. It'll save our backs. It is still two weeks till I will see you and I hate to think about those weeks. I love you. Kiss my babies.

Mitchell

Jan. 30

Dear Mitchell,

Well, your little brother out of all the weekends not to come home chose this one to stay at school. And that poor goat still getting the hots and colds from being stuck in the barn wall. I don't know what to do. It will be another week now till Brice will be home. I can't take the babies out for a walk in this weather to get help. And

I won't let Tom Webster (who's been *kind* enough to come and get my letters and deliver them to the post office) know about this because he would use it as an occasion for spite. I know he would. Momma drove the car up from Decatur and spent the night, but she's of no help whatsoever. She said I should shoot the poor thing. Write back right now and tell me what to do. All in all the goat seems to be taking it very well, but I can't stand to think about him that way. The other goats are starting to nibble on him. Hurry.

Jenny

P.S. Daddy can't come, he's working two shifts.

Feb. 2

Jenny,
  Take a board and hit that animal on the forehead. It won't hurt him. He needs some persuasion. That should knock him back out. Don't shoot him. I'll be home in ten days. It seems like I'm not doing anything but working, eating and sleeping. Be careful. I love you.

Mitchell

Feb. 2

Dear Mitchell,
  I am worried that you didn't get my letter. So I am sending another one just like it. Just in case.
  Well, your little brother out of all the weekends not to come home chose this one to stay at school. And that poor goat still getting the hots and colds from being stuck in the barn wall. I don't know what to do. It will be another week now till Brice will be here. I can't take the babies out in this weather. I won't let Tom Webster, the mailman, help for spite. Momma is her usual helpless

self. She said shoot. The goat's better than me, but others are starting to nibble. Hurry. I think I have remembered it all.

Jenny

Feb. 6

Dear Jenny,

Calm down. If hitting the goat with a 2×4 didn't work, try this. Stop feeding him. You have probably got his neck all swollen, and since you feed and clothe him every day he is fat and happy. Aaron said to build a fire under him. Don't do this. It is just a joke. I will be home soon. I love you.

Mitchell

Feb. 6

Mitchell,

I'm glad that you are going to be home soon because I was afraid to hit him with the board. I might have hit him in the eye or nose. The poor thing he is going on his third week now clutched in the grip of that barn. I have started in with the ax but I only do it a little at a time because the chopping upsets him.

Love, Jenny

P.S. I got a note from Brice and he can't come home this weekend either. Why does he have to study so much?

Feb. 9

My Darling Jenny,

I am writing this as I leave the camp. I will probably get home before this does. But if I don't just leave the goat alone. I hope to God you are talking about using that ax

31

on the barn. I have been so nervous the past two weeks about all of this that I can't sleep. I still love you.

Mitchell

Feb. 9

Mitchell,

This may not get to you before you leave, but you guessed it, the board didn't work. I think you were right about the food too because there are big rolls of fat tight against the barn. I think that I am just going to do nothing else until you get here. I have been so frustrated the last two weeks that I cannot sleep. You better still love me.

Jenny

8

Squirt Harris came pounding round the corner of the porch with a dead cat tied to his belt loop.

"Where'd you get that dead cat, Squirt Harris?" screamed his mother, standing on the porch.

Squirt dug two snow-caked boot heels into the loose snow of the front yard and screamed a great braking automobile screech. The dead cat made two quick orbits at his side. "Found it out in the road, Ma. I didn't kill it, I swear; big truck did." Squirt put one foot on top of the other and slapped at a dog that was sniffing at the cat.

Mrs. Harris was yelling again, "Tom, Tom, come out here and look what the boy's gone and done."

Mr. Harris came out on the porch in his undershirt and said, "Why, he's killed a cat."

And poor Squirt Harris began to fret and whimper. "I didn't kill it, Ma. Promise."

"Well then, you just go put that cat right back out in the road where you found it, you hear?"

"Aw, Ma."

"Now, I said."

"Yes'm."

"And don't get run over yourself."

"Aw, Ma."

"I mean it."

"Yes'm, old fart."

"What?"

"I'm goin', Ma."

Squirt Harris stopped at the ditch before the Decatur Road, untied the cat's tail, crouched low in the gully, bit the cat on its dead ear, gave it a couple of lariat twirls, yelled, "Take this, Kaiser William," and tossed the cat grenadelike onto the road. Then he went to his hidden rock pile to wait on innocent passers-by.

Squirt Harris is known generally as a dirty rock-thrower. You can't walk past the Harris place without that kid pitching a rock at you. And he don't miss much. He's never been known to miss, as a matter of fact. You just count on getting pelted with a rock when you walk past his house, unless it's past his bedtime. And you can't just grab him and wring his little rock-throwing neck because he's just a kid and how'd that look? What's especially bad is he's always trying to surprise you, and just when you think you are safe, zing, a good-sized chunk of creek stone right in the small of your back or at the back of your head. When it's cold he aims for your ears, and you know how that hurts. I'm telling you he's a thoroughly rotten little kid, the kind you swear you'll never raise, surprising you with a smart like an unexpected turn in a story, or an extra step on a staircase.

33

Cars are his specialty. He dents the two left fenders on a car's trip up the Decatur Road and dents the two right ones on the way back down. And you can't find him if you stop and get out. More than that, it's dangerous. You get out and zing, zing, go a couple of fist-sizers, and from somewhere out of the brush mud balls come arching like mortars. It's best just to drive on like nothing happened if you know what's good for you. Why take chances?

His mother tried to stop him, or at least limit his ammunition. She tried to keep him out of range of the road by tying one of his feet to a stake in the yard. That way he could at least play with the dog. Then some of his friends took advantage of his situation and started throwing rocks at him. It was all right, though, the kid eats rocks. Trouble was his momma kept feeding him, with real food, that is, and it only took him six months of growth and working out to be able to reach the road again and ten feet beyond. I'm telling you the boy has a thing for throwing rocks. Born to it. Can kill a cat at fifty feet if he wants to.

He is the Scylla of the Decatur Road. You've got to pass and he knows it and he takes his toll, be you man, woman, machine, or beast.

9

Winter-spring. Dust of midwinter breaking up and free-flowing. The whole world has thawed. But it is a time like that time after a long, shrieking scream: You keep your hands to your ears because the shriek rings in you long after it has stopped; and it could begin again instantly, so fast that you wouldn't have time to save yourself from the hurt of the sound. It is like this. The midwinter cold clings to your lungs during winter-spring thaw, and you know it will freeze again. You leave your coat on when you go out to play with the dog.

It was winter-spring. Dust of midwinter breaking up and free-flowing. And he was plowing. Out in the morning with the winds from the south plowing. And these were his excuses: It was good to turn the earth, the snow to come would better the turned ground, and he had been waiting, he had stood at the door and window since November waiting for a southern wind. And so now he was out with the old dog and the mule and the dirt, and the four of them were working the winter out. "Haw, shump, Number Two, shump," he yelled at the mule, and the mule, Barney Number Two, slanted into the soil and pulled. Young powerful mule, replacement of old Barney, the father's mule.

And old Zeke barked, barked his one deep, resonant bark of the day. The three boys' dog, and now Mitchell's dog. Old, thick, big-pawed, good-souled dog. He didn't need to bark. The dog twice around the mule and the man and then at the man's heels, inspecting the new furrow.

And the ground, like a bell, like black oatmeal, rolling up out of itself. Awesome and expectant. Sure. Like God almost.

And Mitchell, out in the field feeling all alone and somehow heroic, and feeling, at the same time, at home, surrounded, calm. And this is what he was saying, singing: "Haw, shump, Barney, pull, boy," and "Plowing in hope, say, Zeke?" and "All around the water tank, waiting on a train," and preaching, "The sluggard will not plow by reason of the cold, eh, Zeke?" straight out of the almanac, and "*T* for Texas, *T* for Tennessee, *T* for Thelma, that gal that made a wreck out of meeeee." Out in that field plowing with the south wind. "Haw, shump, Number Two, shump. Good mule." And lifting, guiding the hundred-pound plow over and around rocks and sometimes going through them, dancing down the furrow, waltzing with the plow handles, spastic clod-stomping motions to his own music. And the dog, old Zeke, fantastic effort, leaping up at Mitchell's side and snapping at his hat, sprawling back on the ground, four legs in four directions, pausing to lick a clod of dirt. "Rather drink muddy water, sleep in a hollow log." Plowing. Plowing. "You know it, Zeke, we're going to be sick of this come autumn, hunh, boy? But it's all right now, say? I wish I could yodel. Yo de laydy whooo. Sorry, boy. Sorry, Number Two. Shump." Plowing.

Plowing. The acre-and-a-half field bordered by a barbed-wire strand on the high side, and sloping to the Quirks Run on the low side. And time measured by the depth of the plowshare, by the length of the furrow. He had started at eight, and he would finish at three, an acre and a half. And so he went on plowing, set himself in the routine of it, calling "gee," and "haw" at the ends of furrows and the mule turning on his own; Mitchell pressing down on the handles, lifting the blade out of the soil and sliding the plow around to start the next row. Mitchell and the mule and the dog settling down to the work of it. Plowing.

Plowing. Till the plowing becomes like something other than itself, something simpler, like walking or breathing. Till it becomes something that interests your body but leaves the rest of you free. "Haw, shump, Number Two, pull." Till the passings of the furrows take your thoughts away from the immediate present. And he was thinking ahead. Plowing.

Plowing. Perhaps it would be like this: There would be at least twenty-five people, maybe thirty—he and Jenny, Becky, Henry, and little Stephen, who would be a big Stephen by then, and all their kids, and Brice and Stilman

36

would be there too. There would be food all over the place, and screaming and lots of moving around. And afterward, he and Brice and Stilman would go outside and chop wood together, even if they were old men, and they would tell old stories, good stories, and slap each other on the back and maybe they would even cry. Then the women would come out and laugh at them for whatever reason, and each one would touch her husband in her own way. And there would be more stories. Less cussing. And the kids would all be outside, running between the house and the cars (they would have cars by then), screaming until they fell asleep that evening. It would be a big family. It would be good to grow old. And as he came to the end of the furrow, the mule turned toward the barn instead of the next furrow and Mitchell knew it was noon. Knew by the mule and knew because Jenny was leaning on the gate that entered the field, and she was holding his lunch. Noon comes quickly when you are young and plowing. Mitchell left the plow in the field and led the mule to the gate. Jenny had brought lunch for Barney too, a bucket of grain, and Mitchell strapped it to Number Two's head. "Take your time, mule, I'm going to talk to the lady here."

"You were singing, weren't you? I could hear it all the way into the house, even with the baby yelling. Becky and Henry came in and told on your dancing, too. Said Daddy was dancing with Barney all the way down the field. What have you got to say for yourself?"

"Did you bring my lunch out or what?"

"You got fried eggs on bread."

"What happened to this morning's sausage?"

"Gave it to Zeke."

"Well, what in the world did you give it to him for? The dog gets sausage and I get fried eggs."

"Zeke don't like fried eggs," Jenny said.

"Zeke don't like fried eggs?"

"You know Zeke don't like fried eggs."

"He's a dog, for God sakes, an old country retrieving dog. I've seen him steal an egg from a chicken, poke a hole in the end of it with a fang, and suck the insides out raw. Don't like fried eggs."

"There still ain't no sausage. Holler all you want."

"I'm not hollering."

"You don't like fried eggs or what?"

"You know I like fried eggs. I was just thinking sausage all morning. Had my tongue set for sausage."

"Here."

"Thanks."

"When you get done here, I want you to go and help Mr. Webster with his plowing. He's old and needs help."

"He won't let me help."

"You offer anyway."

"I was going to before you even said it."

"I know. Mitchell?"

"Yes?"

"We're having chicken for supper. Get your tongue set for chicken."

"Haw, shump, Number Two, pull, Barney. And you, dog, Zeke, get up from there and walk along here with me. Be my friend all morning knowing you ate my sausage. Don't cock your head at me. Come on along here. Haw, shump, Barney."

And the mule rearing into the furrow, pulling the reins taut, sending a shudder through the plow and through Mitchell's arms. And these were the things that came to him, that he searched after, there in the field with his mule and his dog, plowing, getting his tongue set for chicken. And late that evening, after the big get-together and after the talking, and after beds had been found for everyone, she and he would be alone, and they would tell each other what a good time it had been. And maybe they

38

would whisper about someone, and laugh at someone else. He could imagine her there in the bedroom, standing in her nightgown at the side of the bed. He could imagine her gray hair, and he could imagine soft wrinkles in her cheeks. But he could not think of her being tired. He could not picture her exhausted. And he knew she would be after a day like that. Then he thought about sex, and he laughed, and he wondered, and then he blushed, out there alone in the field. He looked at Zeke to see if he was being watched. The dog was cradled in a furrow, getting dirt-clean. He thought about holding her, and falling asleep. Plowing.

Plowing. The children, there were three now—Becky and Henry were two and a half, and the baby, Stephen, was eight months. My Lord, there would be more. Perhaps, when the boys were old enough to help, the family would own two mules. And there would be this same field fallow. He looked all around himself, planning the field and the future out. Yes, he would take one mule, the new one, let them use Number Two, and start at the up-slope side of the field. The boys could start in the middle of the field, halfway down the hillside. And they would race to see who could finish their half first. He would race his boys. They would probably be eager, planning out who was going to start and who finish. He would have to holler and boast a lot. And they would probably win. They would probably win on their own. Becky would be cheering for her daddy and Jenny would yell for her boys. And when it was all over and the two boys were strutting around and talking and the women were laughing, he would simply say, "You had the better mule," and they would say no, and laugh some more, so he would have to rush them, chase them all four down to the Quirks Run and push them in, clothes and all. He planned it out, plowing in hope. Plowing.

Plowing. And amid this and on the tail of it, as he and

the dog and mule began the last few rows, something else came to him. It consisted of two quick images, one of his father dying, and another of his brother Stilman riding some train to some new work. He frowned at the first image but cringed at the second. He saw himself in his father's eyes, and he knew by the cringe that he himself had given up so many possibilities. And then he saw himself running alongside a moving train. It was a strange thought for him, and he didn't like it. So he concentrated on the plowing, putting extra weight on the handles so the blade would dip farther into the black earth. He stopped once, and picked up an arrowhead. But he finished before long, finished and put up the gear and the mule; gave the mule a pat on the flank and said, "Good mule." He came back out of the barn, and began stepping along the furrows toward the house. The dirt was good dirt. In the row closest to the house he found Henry sitting in a furrow, his legs covered over with earth. The boy was packing his navel with dirt. And so Mitchell heaved a great sigh, and laughed out loud, and plucked his son, as you would a turnip, from the winter-spring furrow. He thought of Mr. Webster as he carried the boy home, and he looked at his watch. It was still early.

10

If you are walking on the Decatur Road when winter turns spring, you will probably slip and fall and hurt yourself. It is a mud-happy stretch at this turn, and if you are not careful you could very well slide all the way into Decatur, could very well bump your bottom on the steps of the Decatur courthouse. The road is full of a thousand mini-runs at this time, etching wrinkles in the ruts, carrying off the topsoil to the Quirks Run and the Muskatatuck. Regan Williams, ex-county surveyor, says the Decatur Road dropped four inches during his tenure, 1908–1929, says one of these days the first nine miles of the road will bottom out at clay or slate and the water off the knobs will take the Decatur Road instead of the Quirks Run. We will have to take the Quirks Run ourselves, he says. Some poor fellow, says Regan Williams, will have to go back and change all of the maps to read the Quirks Road and the Decatur Run one of these days. Won't that confuse 'em, God bless us all, says Regan Williams. Regan gets carried away sometimes. But he is basically right. These knobs are in a flattening process right now. Someday, some poor fellow will have to go back and change all of the maps so they will read Appalachian Knobs and Thacher Plains.

But all of that is neither here nor now. The springtime is a good time for finding arrowheads on the Decatur Road. The water that carries off the topsoil leaves the flint behind and shines it up besides. The road is littered with the marks and remnants of 24,000 years of lousy bow-and-arrow shots. Shots that missed the bird or the rabbit and lost themselves in the underbrush and dirt of the animal path that would become the Decatur Road. It is an embarrassing legacy. You are almost ashamed to stoop over and pick an arrowhead up. You hide them in your pockets until you get home. But, my Lord, can you imagine all of the bullets, the buckshot, they will find after we are gone? And we don't even go looking after our missed shots.

It takes a good half hour to make a mile on the Decatur Road in the mud. The mile or so from the Harris place to the Holland shack is especially slow. The road leans a bit there, and it is hard to keep your balance. Wagons are

41

always sliding into trees or the creek and people are always cussing at their heavy boots. But what can you say? You know the summer is coming. You know the dry road is coming. You can say the Decatur Road is made of dirt. It is a road of seasons. You can say that.

11

It was something else, something other. And Mitchell, when he heard, would think it was odd, what she had done: Stepping out of the bed only a day after giving birth, saying, "I am going for a walk," and her mother looking up and calling, "But you've got nothing on, and no shoes," but she not even turning, not even saying goodbye, just walking out into the dusk-evening. He would think it odd.

And wasn't it strange, she thought. But it had chased her out. It had chased her out as if she hadn't a will of her own. All of a sudden she had needed to be out of the house; it was crowded with just one person in a room. But now it turned on her, as the thing always did when she had it. She felt lonely. She had walked hard for five minutes, out of the yard and into the woods, without daring to try to sort it out yet, and now she was lonely. She needed to be with people. But then she didn't know again. It was confusing. She would need to be or do one thing and the complete opposite of it all at the same time. So she just stood still. That seemed to be as sensible a thing as any. If you could stand still, you could start with that.

She stopped at an open sandy spot next to the Quirks Run, where a little wave arched up after a rock and made a perfect half-circle water-fan, shot through with moonlight. It was full night now. It was quiet. Even the stream made no noise. There was fog creeping in, dropping and crawling in and by and drawing back. And then there was the wind, slight, that caused the just-budding branches to slap against each other, and made her nightgown cling to her legs. The moon was almost full. But it was still there, the indefinable thing, that was something like waiting, that was something like not knowing whether to hold on or let go, but wasn't either of these at all. It was something else, something other.

So she just stood there, looking at the stream, and listening for the night. And it began to frustrate her, the standing still, as if it weren't enough, and so she cupped her breasts in her hands through the white cotton and lifted them up.

She began to walk again, along the Quirks Run up into the steeper hills, a white shadow among the underbrush. She gathered the loose folds of cloth tightly in front of her and pushed the brush away, her hand white and quick as a bird's wing. And she began to cry, feeling there was some decision to be made but not knowing what the decision, or even the problem, was. It was wet underfoot; she could feel the wet earth seeping through her socks. She paused and looked down at them, still crying, looking at the thick, bright red man's socks she had on, because her feet had been cold in the bed. And the sight of them made her laugh and made her stop crying. But then it returned, the thing that made her feel in-between, and so she cried again, but even that did not help this time.

There were moon shards scattered over the wet-leaved ground. And the silence still there. She looked at the moon, trying to make out the dark side, make the moon a full circle, and she thought that she did, that she could, and then she didn't. And suddenly she noticed a silhouette against a glowing sycamore: a squirrel's head, jutting in and out of its hole high on the trunk, tentatively taking steps out on a branch and then drawing back. But then, after it had drawn back in and waited there for a few moments, and she had thought to go on, it shot out of the hole along the branch at what must have been top speed, careening to the very end of the branch and not stopping there but leaping out, leaping and not falling but flying, all four of his legs stretched out wide, and the squirrel flying across the open space through the night, silhouette across the moon, to another sycamore branch and along that branch into another hole. As if it were a first test of spring, she thought. And she made a small jump herself from one flat rock to another.

She was still following the Quirks Run. As she came to forks in the creek, she always chose the larger branch, following it to the next fork. She passed through a fir thicket and across a small open meadow where the water spread out into a small glassy pool. The three-quarter moon was a streak on it and the sight of it frightened her for a moment. She had the thought that perhaps it was the moon that was the reflection and that all the light in the night came from this pool before her. The idea of throwing a rock into it came to her, and she picked up a stone and swung it underhand high into the night toward the pond. But she lost it in the darkness and instead of the splash she waited for she heard only a dull thump and the chirping of a cricket. She knew you could never find a chirping cricket, no matter how hard you looked.

Immediately after the pool, the creek became much narrower and faster, her climb rockier and steeper. She rose up through sycamores and poplars and old elms to pine seedlings and a thick blue-spruce forest, where the creek gurgled down granite and quartz steps. There was no grass here, just the bed of needles and outcroppings of stone. The moon was clear and colder somehow among the fir, and closer, somehow more inviting and dangerous, so that she wanted to climb until she couldn't go any farther. She took to the creek itself, stepping up the moss-covered stones, till the creek ceased to flow, but still shone in the moonlight, as if the rocks were sweating. She was at the top of the knob now and she turned around and sat on a rock in the midst of the creek/waterfall. She shone as if she were a small white light in the sky. She could see forever: the dark mountains to the east and the knobs all around her, sloping gradually to the west. And it surprised her, the lights far down below her, when she realized they came from her house. It seemed so small to hold so much. The field around the black space of the barn was a white veil and the house was a little white spot down in a well. She felt a drop of water on her shoulder where a brier had torn her nightgown. Up above her, out of a seemingly solid piece of granite, drops of water were forming. She watched, and it seemed to take an eternity for a drop to become full and bulbous, and then it would linger for a few eternities longer before it broke itself away from the small crack in the granite and fall, a tiny spark in the darkness, the six inches to her shoulder. She watched the process to completion four times, letting each drop fall on her shoulder, shriekingly cold. She caught the fifth in her hand and drank it.

And she decided she could say this at least: "This creek called the Quirks Run, which runs past my house and nine miles farther into the Muskatatuck, starts at this point, begins here, and then makes of itself what it does." She could say this, and that was something. And she decided that there were some things in this world that no two people could understand at the same time. And she thought some more and she thought, no, that was not it, that was not it at all; what it was, was her fear that nothing would ever happen—that brought her here, brought her to need this evening. And as she thought, she felt there was something sifting through the woods, something original. There was a voice calling through the night. And the word was "Jenny" it called. It was her husband looking for her. It was Mitchell. But, for a moment, when she first made the connection between herself and the word, between this voice calling her name and her presence to hear it, it seemed to her to be somehow the most extravagant treasure and coincidence. Almost as if it were unusual.

12

No one has anything to do with him.

He came tumbling out of a boxcar during the spring of 1919, walked—rumpled and somehow arrogant—along the Decatur Road into town. He went straight to the courthouse; he walked down the center of the street. Once a car had to swerve to miss him. He went into the courthouse, and then he came right back out of it. No time in there at all, really. He came right back out and started walking back the same way he'd come. But when he gets to the train crossing he just keeps on walking. And he walks that way, right in the middle of the Decatur Road, for another twenty-seven miles: past the Daniels place, over the Muskatatuck, past Perry's Landing Store, to the old Holland shack. So everyone figured he paid off the taxes on the place and meant to farm it. That's what everyone figured.

So he moves into the shack and he doesn't do anything. He doesn't work on the house or clear any ground. He doesn't even clean the place up. What he does is start taking in stray dogs. It was queer. In the evenings you could see him in a chair by the window, holding two or three dogs in his lap. Dogs all over the place before long.

It got even funnier when he never left the farm. He didn't even go to the store. People started wondering. John Perry left his store one day and went into Decatur just to find out who this guy was. He was another Holland. That surprised everyone because he didn't look like any of the Hollands who left the place in 1910. This guy was short and stocky, had just a ring of hair on his head. Maybe he was thirty-five. The Hollands who left in 1910 were all tall and thin, and none of them had ever been bald. They left because they got a lot of money from some relative. They were going to Montana. So this man didn't fit at all.

After a while the shack and the yard started to look pretty bad. He had put up a fence around the place with anything he could find and the dogs trampled all the grass to dirt. The house was supported by columns of stacked rocks and you could see all the way under it to the back-yard. You could see where the dogs had pawed out pits to keep cool. There were boards, limbs, rocks and old bones scattered all over. The roof of the house was missing shingles. The bottom half of the screen door had no screen. And he never left that place, as far as anyone knew, in the daytime. Neither he nor the dogs seemed to gain any weight, but then again, they didn't get any thinner, either. It's still the same way.

John Perry was always curious about the guy, mistrusted him. He drove up and down the Decatur Road one day, stopped at each farm and asked if they were missing any chickens or anything from the garden. No one was missing anything. Perry worried about Holland because Perry was the tax collector in that part of the county and would have to go get money from Holland someday. How could the guy have any money? Besides this, there was the guy himself. No one really knew him. In fact, no one even got physically close to him. The fence around the shack had no gate. How could you trust a guy who wouldn't talk to you? But Perry got his money. Holland left it clipped to the screen door of Perry's Store one night. Nothing came of that.

Vardy Cummins, who has the place a mile down the Decatur Road from Holland's, did see Holland away from the shack once. Cummins was out at midnight hunting with one of his boys. They were on the top of a knob and had taken a shot at a coon. The coon was hit, but only wounded. It fell out of the tree and took off down the knobside. Cummins and his boy fell in after it, running headlong down the grade, the boy carrying the lamp. They caught up with the coon down in the gully. Cummins raised his gun and told the boy to raise the lamp. The boy did that, and there in the outer fringe of the light was Holland, with seven or eight of his dogs all around him. The dogs stayed put. Cummins said Holland just waved a hand and the dogs stayed put. The coon walked slowly, dripping blood, between them. Between Cummins with his gun and Holland with his dogs. It disappeared into a hole at the base of a tree.

13

"Okay, now, what is that?"

And the boy Henry, perched on his father's shoulders, said, "A hickory, and you make things out of 'em, like baskets and gun handles."

"And that one there?"

"Locust, and you use 'em for fence posts 'cause they don't rot."

Mitchell pointed at another tree.

"I don't know."

"Sure you do. It's a poplar. They just look a little different in the early spring."

"There are some things too big for any of us to understand, Mr. Parks. Too big. The world is full of mystery. So we must trust. And our trust, even though we give it, is a debt, a debt owed to Christ. Your mother knew this. She was a good Christian woman, though long gone. I think you and your family ought to be at church this Sunday. I came out here myself just to extend this invitation." The Reverend Edwards was walking behind Mitchell. His face was the mottled brown color of a chicken bone an hour or two after the meal.

"You keeping a lookout for that goat, Henry?"

"Yes, but I haven't seen her yet, Pa."

"That's okay, you keep looking; we'll find her."

"He's a fine-looking boy, Mr. Parks. Knows his woods."

"Yes, sir. You're gonna be like one of those big sycamores on the Muskatatuck when you grow up, aren't you, son?"

"Yep."

"See that goat?"

"Nope."

"Sorry to have you out in the woods like this, Reverend. This goat that's lost is about to bear, and I need to find her before dark. I think that's why she run off, 'cause she's gonna bear."

"We must care for the ladies, mustn't we?" And the Reverend brought his eyes up to level. "You know, Mrs. Edwards does half my work. She talks with the wives while I speak to the men. I can reach more folks that way. She knows the Bible as well as I, almost."

"Jenny was raised on it. Mrs. Edwards and her will get along, I suppose."

"Good to hear it. Like I was saying, Mr. Parks, we all have this debt, and we all must make account. And the best way to show we are paying on the ledger sheet is by going into the Lord's house every Sunday and meeting with others like ourselves to praise and learn of Him. It's only natural."

"The kids are awful young to be walking all that way to the church every Sunday. See that goat, Henry?"

"Nope. Pa, Momma says we oughta go to the church."

"You really ought to listen to your wife, Mr. Parks. She seems to understand . . ."

"Over there!" And Henry almost fell off his father's shoulders. "Pa, on the rocks over there. She's laying down. She's sick."

"Here, son, get down. She's not sick. My Lord, goat, give up your straw for a rock. She won't be long at all, boys. Look here, Henry. Look, the baby goat's being born. Here, son, help. Hold its head up off the ground as it comes. Looky here, looky here. It won't hurt you; help her, here."

The Reverend pushed in, "Son, let me . . ."

"Please, let the boy, mister."

"Pa, it's opening its eyes right here in front of me."

"Hold it up, and when I tell you, you pull real easy on its shoulders. Watch her, son. Okay, now, pull real easy. Good. There. Now let go of him, let him alone."

"Pa, look at our hands."

"Just get you some dirt between your palms and rub. It won't hurt you."

"It's a wonderful and mysterious thing, isn't it, Mr. Parks? Amazing."

"Yes, sir."

"Simply amazing."

"Yes, sir." And Mitchell stepped back, laying his hands upon the boy's shoulders.

"We really would like to have you and the wife and children with us Sunday. The sermon will be on sharing this Sunday, and . . ."

"Well, I've talked it over with my wife, and she and the kids will go to your church. They'll all go to the Sunday school, but the kids won't go to the sermon. It's nothing personal. I just don't want anybody scaring them. Now, we need to let the baby find its momma; let's sit down here and be quiet for a while."

"Hello? Mrs. Parks?"

"Yes? In here. Oh, Mrs. Edwards. We were expecting you, but not quite this soon. Is the Reverend here? I don't know where Mitchell's wandered off to."

"Oh, he's with Mr. Edwards. I didn't mean to interrupt. Please go on with your milking."

"Well, I do need to finish. She gets upset when you leave her half-full. Becky, bring Stephen and Sarah over here and sit down. Leave Mrs. Edwards alone. Come on."

"Have you had a chance to speak with your husband about coming to church, Mrs. Parks?"

"Yes, ma'am. The children and I will begin this Sunday. Mitchell thinks he needs to stay at home. I was hoping the Reverend might convince him to come."

"What do you suppose it is, Mrs. Parks? Is he a communist?"

"Oh, no, ma'am. He just wasn't raised with it. He and his brothers stopped going to church when their mother died. I started to read the Bible to the children here the other day, and Mitchell listened too, but after I read just a little ways he got up and went out to the barn."

"Why was that?"

"There's a part where it says the ground is cursed. I think he had the idea that was the silliest thing he ever heard."

"Well, he has a family. It's his responsibility, not yours, to keep them together, especially on the Sabbath. It's almost a sin, him breaking up the family like that."

51

"Please come in the house, Mrs. Edwards. I need to put the kids to bed. Come on, kids, time for bed; look, it's dark already."

"Can we have some milk and a cookie?"
"And some cedar in the stove?"
"Yes, yes, come on; get in bed first."
"Momma, Stephen's hoggin' all the covers."
"Stephen, you roll over and be good. Now, I don't want to hear any fighting. I'll be back in a minute."
And she was back in a minute, putting cedar chips into the stove and giving each of them a cup of milk.
"Where's the cookies?"
"In my pocket; hold your horses."
"I can smell the cedar smoke already. Momma, I love cedar smoke."
"Momma, tell Becky to stop sniffin' like that."
"Becky."
"How come Henry don't have to go to bed now?"
"He's with your father, Stephen. He'll be back in a little while. Don't you stick your tongue out at me. Just try that again."
And the boy did, and Jenny put a cookie on it. Then Becky and Sarah copied.
"Now, go to sleep, all of you, and be quiet."

It was the reflection off a spring-blue new moon rising up behind the trees on top of the ridge that made them notice the large abalone-inlaid crucifix dangling from Mrs. Edwards' neck, the cross so heavy it pressed down the cloth of her dress between her breasts.

They were in the front yard, the four of them, next to the little black car the Edwards had driven up in. It was chilly, and Mrs. Edwards crossed her arms. The Reverend looked away from the crucifix and rubbed the fender of his car.

Mitchell was standing with his back to the moon, looking like an old stump, his hands shoved in his pockets. He said, "I want to thank you folks for coming out."

And Jenny moved over and put her arm around him, her dress fluttering in the slight breeze. She said, "Yes."

And the Reverend: "Then we will at least see you and the children this Sunday, Mrs. Parks?"

"No, I don't think so. I'm sorry."

And Mitchell had a little pause in the beating of his life.

She spoke, and the sound of her voice was as the shaking of a leaf. And she standing there, not turning and walking to the house as she easily could have done, as it would have been her perfect right to do, but standing there and looking at them. She saying, "I won't have God coming between us. No."

14

It was a good sound: the consistent grating of the trowel on the mortar. And it was a great irony, the perfectness of the dam; it was the first thing he had ever been in on from start to finish, the building of it, and there was something of pride there. He had looked through the surveyor's glass himself and seen the straight line, and he had set the level in thirty different places, in all four directions, and the bubble always centered.

But the dam itself, as far as the act of blowing it up tonight was concerned, was nothing. It was the eight men who counted, getting them worked up and involved. Once they did the thing, they would be part of the whole movement. It would keep them honest and active in the movement. The dam was insignificant.

The men, they weren't a spineless lot like you ran up against sometimes; they were just ordinary fellows who had never thought about their situation before and needed a little prodding. But, God, they had been ripe. This job had been one of the smoothest yet. It had been a stroke of genius, looking for the right kind of atmosphere and mood of men in this outfit. No one had ever thought of it before, and when he got back to Chicago and told them all how easy it had been, they would go wild. He had known that these men building the dam must have been a dissatisfied and angry lot if they were working for this outfit. It was only reasonable. So he got hired on himself, and he talked to the men—at lunch, at break, on the job and after; he told them that before long the dams, dams like this one, would be used by the government like everything else—just like the big coal companies and the auto works—all the money going to the already rich, but the poor man with kids, the guy who actually sweats building the dam, would get nothing.

At first they were hesitant, as good men should have been (except for the Singleton kid, who was a lazy-no-good on the job, who always said yes right on time; he was either crazy or a liar; he would have to be watched until the thing was done). They had worked on the dam for months, from cutting down the trees to rechanneling the Quirks Run to actually troweling the mortar, as he was doing now. The dam would be finished today and the men paid. For a while the men had held on to the dam, as if it were some kind of pretty car they were giving up. They thought it was a shame to destroy what they had worked months on. It was almost a work of art, curving gracefully across the gap between two knobs, symmetrical and smooth and strong. It made a three-acre pond, almost fifty feet deep at the dam. It wasn't a Hoover, but it was a thing they had done. The men talked for hours one afternoon, as they stood on the scaffolding on the outer wall of the dam, about the old man who had come up the Decatur Road with a bucket and dumped a four-pound bass into the pond off the dam. The men had all clapped and said they would catch that fish if they had to work at it for ten years. And he himself had looked at the blueprints of the dam one day and thought that at least these would survive and another dam could be built.

But the men had come around to him at last. These men were like the water, if they ran free they were simply feckless, but if you could hold them together, that was the beauty of it, if you could hold them together you could move mountains—a controlled force aimed at food for everybody and shoes and shirts for everybody. You just needed to hold them together. And he was holding them. He was like this mortar, holding the dam together and channeling all that power of the water to good.

It was surprisingly easy how he had done it. To hold the eight men together he had simply charged each one with bringing something they would need tonight. He would bring the dynamite himself, and Jones (he could trust him more than any of them) would bring the caps, and Singleton a shovel, Walker the wire, and so on. They would all be here tonight, and it was going to work; he could feel it.

He stepped easily along the scaffolding, smoothing over some rough spots along the dam's upper edge. He looked over at Jones and winked, and Singleton, who was the third man on the scaffolding crew, broke out in a laugh. The two supervisors of the job looked up from their blueprints spread on the tailgate of a pickup and smiled. They were happy to be finished too. Then, as he leaned over from his station to tell Jones that by this time tomorrow they would be in Chicago eating char-broil and potatoes, Singleton forgot where he was and stepped over to hear what was being said. The scaffolding tipped, and it was he who was falling, not Singleton or even Jones, who could have been spared, but he himself, and as he fell he knew, more than he knew the physicality of his own falling, that he had lost, that he had lost them, that the whole thing was shot, so that the impact became only an anticlimax. They were still up there, Singleton and Jones, reaching their hands down to him, but it was as if he were far underwater, it was as if he had fallen on the other side of the dam wall and were deep underwater, and he could do nothing but look up in wonder and novelty. And perhaps he could have caught hold of Jones' sleeve as they picked him up from the rocks, told Jones to go on with the thing and how, and maybe they would have; but how tell him how? He was deep underwater, he was the bass, sleek and dark at the bottom of the pond, and if he spoke they would only see bubbles at the surface. And as they carried him up the steep hillside he had the full realization that he was all broken inside, and as the two WPA supervisors took him from the men and lifted him into the bed of the truck he suddenly felt, and was overcome by, the complete and gentle inevitability of the world.

15

This is what they had told each other two summers after they were married: It is a simple thing. We will buy this piece of land adjoining the farm; we will take the three hundred dollars I have saved and you have saved and make a down payment and take out a twenty-year loan. The tobacco base itself will make half the payment if we lease it out, and we can rent the house on the land; and when our boys come fourteen or fifteen we will farm both farms ourselves, and when they are married this extra piece of land will be theirs, the children's. And the brothers, Brice and Stilman, who were away but who owned the farm equally with Mitchell, said yes, it was a good idea, said mortgage the farm for Henry and the sons to come.

"Yes, Mr. Parks, we can do business, I think," said Justin Caldwell. "Now, your property, Mr. Parks, what percentage level ground? Have you got water on the place? Any erosion? How many acres are cleared? What kind of house? Outbuildings? Sounds very good. A twenty-year mortgage will do you fine, get the adjoining property paid for before you know it. This is the rate of interest you'll be paying, and this figure here represents your yearly payment, due one week following the sale of your tobacco. You're getting a deal on this property. I would say the base leased out will net you half of your payment. And the property has an old house on it. Rent that out. Well, let's shake on this thing; the papers make things legal, still I like to shake on it. Then I'll see you come market time. See me if there's any trouble at all. Good day."

Mitchell Parks, stepping out of the bank into the morning sun, his face letting go of concentration and becoming stupid-looking to the degree that little children point. Mitchell Parks, running the first three miles back up the Decatur Road toward home.

And in the evening on Sundays, after what work there was to be done on the home farm, Mitchell would walk over the hill a little ways to the piece of property that was to be the children's. And he would walk over it, to learn the trees and the springs and the rocks as he knew them on the home farm, so that to him an acre of it meant not so many square yards but so many yellow poplars or so much loam. And if old man Tucker (it was the old man and his wife who rented the house and worked the tobacco) was out in the field working, Mitchell would stop and say hello and maybe help out. Sometimes Jenny would go too, and Mitchell would point things out to her, saying this stump will have to come up, that grove there thinned (and did you see that rabbit?), and these rocks picked up out of this field. And later, as the children came, they would all walk the land, and Jenny and Mitchell would tell them these same things, in the evening on Sundays.

But it was the funniest thing: Mitchell slouched back in a chair at the kitchen table and Jenny, across the table, leaning forward out of her chair and resting on her fore-arms. And between them, on the oak table (the table grained and heavy and scarred), lay the salt and pepper shakers, plus the eleven dollars left over from the sale of the tobacco and the payment of the year's note. And Jenny says, "Well, we will just have to work harder."

After nearly coming up short, it occurred to him that he could no longer share. On the days when the corn or the goats or the tobacco needed no care, he would take his saw and his rifle into the woods. It occurred to him that the most important thing was the support of the soil: its firmness under his step and under his house, its food for his family. And this made him realize that what he had always thought of as the land before was not just the land, but the animals and the trees and the birds. And now the land itself was the only important thing, the soil, and he couldn't afford to lose it; he couldn't afford to share. And so he would take his crosscut on one shoul-der and his gun on the other. He would do this in the morning. And in the evening he would come home, hitch up the mule to the sled and go back into the woods. And finally, he would come home with a load of what he called his "selfishness": a cord of firewood that he could sell for a dollar, and the skins of animals, supple and smooth, freshly scraped.

And they were at the table again, almost in no time, but this time there was no eleven dollars. Instead there was the pink sheet of paper marked "Insufficient," and, stapled to it, a smaller white sheet of grace stamped "Extension Granted."

At lunch and dinner, before Mitchell would come in, Jenny would gather the children in the kitchen and remind them to be quiet at the table, not to interrupt their father, or to ask him too many questions. She would say, "He will just have to tell you no, and that would make him sad." And they would say, "Okay, Momma," and look at her and then at each other. Then she would put them at the table, and instead of calling Mitchell from the kitchen door, she would walk out to him in the field. As often as not he would simply say "No," or "Later." But when he did stop, let himself be knocked out of his intense purpose by her voice and presence, the walk back to the house and the children gave him, and her, the time to work him out of his anger, his fury of helplessness.

It was Sunday evening, and it was the old man, Tucker, who was crossing over the hill toward the Parks place. Jenny saw him first, saw him stepping carefully over the field. And she called Mitchell from the other room and told him, "Don't let him come all this way."

And Mitchell said, "He's got what he can pay in his hand."

And Jenny: "Don't make him come all the way in here in front of me. And make sure he keeps enough for them. It's not his fault he can't pay any more than it's ours."

Mitchell walked out to the old man in the field, and the first thing he did was shake the old man's hand and ask him if he would do him a favor and help set a gate that was leaning. It would take two.

And at night, after the children were in bed, they would talk about possibilities.

She said, "What if I worked the tobacco? Henry could

59

help me. And you took a job with that WPA? What about that?"

And Mitchell said, "What about the other kids? We got more kids."

"Momma. I could get Momma to come during the day and help out. She might have to spend the night sometimes."

"Would she do that?"

"Yes."

"You've already asked her?"

"Yes."

"You know you are letting yourself in for more grief than I am."

"We'll get along."

"If the crop prices drop again, even the WPA money won't be enough."

"We can't not do this."

"All right."

The moon was near full, so they did not need to carry the lamps tonight. They moved slowly through the rows of the young tobacco plants, their hoes swinging in quick, careful arcs, the blade flashing with the moonlight. They would reach the end of a row and scrape the dew-mud from their shoes and one or the other would say, "Go inside, I'll finish," and the other would laugh; it came to be a joke. Then they went to the next row, knifing weeds out of the darkness. And the dew would drop on them as they worked, drop until they came into the house. She would then say, "I will have breakfast in a little bit," as he came into the lamplit brooding kitchen buttoning his WPA shirt. And he would say back, "We can't keep this up forever."

Mitchell stepped into the Perry's Landing Store to listen to the market prices coming over the radio. And it

60

happened for the fourth year in a row, the drop in prices, and before he stepped back out onto the Decatur Road he told the men in the store that the whole goddamned country was falling apart.

"Jenny, I'd sell some of the place, but no one would buy it. I wrote Brice and Stilman."

"You think they'll come?"

"They don't need to. I'm sure they knew it was coming as well as us. It's a dirty thing to do to them."

"It wasn't your fault."

"I tell you, a fellow gets desperate."

"When will we have to move?"

"Note's due after we sell the crop. We'll have to move a week after, I suppose."

"It wasn't our fault."

"Here, I bought the kids some candy when it came over the radio."

"You're the fourth one this week, Mr. Parks. The bank's got no choice. But no, Mr. Parks, we don't want you off the farm. It's a very simple thing. Mr. Parks, we're going to let you rent."

16

The Minister Washer, in a narrow-lapeled black suit coat, leans back against the pickled okra jar in the Perry's Landing Store with a look of blatant disbelief on his face and says, "Aw, go directly to hell; you don't say?"

And Bob Perry, John Perry's fourth son, says yes, yes, he had heard it from Mort Norton with his own two ears, and there wasn't no more truth to it than a Ford having good brakes.

"Will somebody turn down the music coming out of that box! Drives me crazy," says Wilson Fellers, and he gives a frown.

"I'd like a sack of flour and some of that facial cream, Mr. Perry, and put it on my account." Then Mrs. Sorly takes her bag and walks real slow and pretend-refined out of the store.

Wilson Fellers, who never misses a chance, leans over to Washington Turner and says, "She didn't have to tell me that facial cream was on her account."

Washington Turner says back, "If you don't like that music, why are you tapping your foot?"

"You kids get out of them crackers," yells old John Perry. "Durn kids."

"Even out of the goodness of his heart?" opines the minister.

"He ain't got no goodness in his heart," Bob Perry says.

Then Whip Jordan, who is like a bad pill to take, said, "He ran out of goodness in 1932. Didn't kick this three-legged dog that limped in front of him." And he adds, "Haw, haw, haw."

"Aw, go straight to hell and back," the minister throws in.

"Speaking of that"—this is John Perry—"you remember that fella that got killed working on the dam up yonder last year; they going to put up a brass plaque in his honor naming the dam after him. It's gonna be called the G. W. Nedlaw State Water Conservatory. Damn long name for such a puny dam if you ask me."

"Who'd ever want a dam named after you? Every time somebody'd call your name they'd damn you out of habit," says Wilson Fellers, "I wonder how much that brass would be worth melted down."

"Joo hear about that lady in Decatur shootin' a cow?"
Bob Perry, who fancies himself a cosmopolitan, says.

"No," so many people throw in, it's no use telling you
their names.

But then Mrs. Sorly comes back in, livid, saying John
Perry gave her cornmeal instead of flour but it was all
right, she could understand such a jackass mistake.

Wilson Fellers says just loud enough to be heard in
China, "Ought to throw in an extra jar of that facial cream
for the mistake, John."

"Lazy drunk," she calls him.

"Spit and spunk, give us a kiss." He winks at her.

Then the minister says, "All right, all right."

And Johnson Daniels, the mediator, tells us all, "Well,
you know, either he's a lazy drunk or she's spit and spunk,
one or t'other."

And then Whip Jordan nods, so Johnson put his pipe
back in his mouth.

And all of a sudden Ben Pokker, who's been sitting over
in the corner next to the stove, wakes up and starts crying, saying, "I have never had anything that was good all
the way through: horses, houses, guns, women. My dog's
only got one eye and he is always squinting out of that
one."

So John Perry, showing a heart, throws him a bottle of
orange pop and that shuts him up.

"Well," the Minister Washer adds to another conversation, "I don't believe that would be murder in the eyes of
God."

And somebody, you don't know who, says, "Well, that's
all I needed to know."

Washington Turner, on the subject of Frank Spicer,
returns, "He ain't got no brains."

"I think that boy's zipper is stuck," Bob Perry agrees,
"but that Hily, she's something, ain't she?"

Then all the men laugh and smile at the same time,

talking about Hily Spicer and that spit curl she does on
one of her temples.

And just when you think they're never going to shut up,
this little boy comes in from the windy spring and asks,
"Why don't a bird's eye tear?"

17

The first storm of spring. Clouds coming over the hollow
and settling like the folds of a black chiffon dress falling
to the floor. And the wind and rain, all at once. There are
old leaves blowing across the yard, and occasionally one
will slap up against a post on the front porch, wet and
brown-black, and stick there for a still moment. Up in the
hills, drops of water are running off new leaves and falling
to the ground.

Mitchell is sitting on the porch with Jenny, watching.
"Here," he says, "feel the drops, they're warm. This rain
is from Texas, I bet." And he rubs his face with the drops
of water and yawns. It is early morning.

She had never had to contend with a drunk man before.
Her father had liked a drink once in a while; she could
remember smelling it on his breath when he came home
late from work. But that was nothing like this. The only
thing she could think of to do was to be mad and let him
know it. Her mother had said to send the children to her
and to shame him when they were gone. But she couldn't
do that. She felt anger, not vengeance, and shaming him
would be like shaming herself. She would hurt more than
he for it.

Mitchell had never been drunk before. And now it was
the third time in two weeks. And a fight last night. Whip
Jordan had come riding up on a mule and said, "Mrs.

Parks, Mitchell's got into a fight at Perry's Store. Come with me if you'd like." And so she took her dishtowel back in the house, told the children not to go off, and mounted the mule behind Whip. They met Mitchell and two other men halfway down the Decatur Road. The men tipped their hats and backed off, saying "so long" to Mitchell.

"Are you hurt?" she asked.

"My mouth hurts a little bit, but I'm all right, honey."

And she said, "Don't call me that."

"Well."

They walked the rest of the way home, Mitchell saying, "Excuse me," and running off into the woods twice.

He turned around and leaned against one of the porch posts. He said to her, "Did you read the part in the letter about Stilman being able to see the night coming from far off? It must be awful flat land there in Texas. Not like here at all." And he was quiet.

And by now, up in the hills, the drops of water were gathering, forming tiny rivulets between the pine needles and old acorn shells. Across the hollow a dead limb snapped and fell into the edge of the plow field. One of the air vents on the barn is clapping.

"They don't grow tobacco there in Texas, you know. Grow cotton. Warm most of the time, he said."

She almost couldn't hear him for the rain. But she did, and she pretended not to. Then that was it. Or at least part of it. It was the letter from Stilman that he had gotten a while back. She almost wished Stilman and Brice wouldn't write. They both wandered, and Mitchell got a letter from each of them every month or so. Stilman's came from West Virginia coal mines, Montana logging camps, and now Texas, wherever he could get a job cooking. Brice had joined a group of American pilots in China after he graduated and got out of the service. They were fighting the Japanese, and the letters that got through came soiled and torn. Mitchell couldn't sit down and read them. In one letter Brice said they needed a baling-wire mechanic like Mitchell, and he had been depressed for two days. And now that the farm wasn't his anymore, she watched the arrival of the letters with something like anguish.

"I'm sorry," he said, scratching at the post, "I've just needed to think about these things."

And the rills and rivulets make thousands of little V's in the soil, carrying off the debris of the winter, dust of winter. The storm rises and subsides, rises and subsides. Rain rolls off the tin roof of the house and splats into its own pockets in the ground. Everything ceaselessly gravitates to the ocean. The Quirks Run rises, and a small stick floats swiftly away. And there a clear blue bottle, neck up, gorgeous.

"I saw fires yesterday, Mitchell," she says. "Some people think it's time to seed the tobacco beds."

He shook his head slowly—yes. And she saw what the other part was. He was tired. And several things almost came to her mind but she stopped them, and suddenly with intensity, looking at the raindrops, she wondered what you can say to someone who is tired. Then she tried to say something else, and still nothing came to her. So she gave in. She conceded to him the right to be tired.

Mitchell said, "Sometimes I am afraid of myself."

And she said, "Me, too. I mean I'm afraid of myself sometimes, too."

"I think about things I've got no right in the world to think about. Like going away from here. You know, just going. And it's worse lately."

"Does owning the land mean that much?"

"It was the losing it. It's that Daddy owned it. If he or I had never had it, it would be different."

"Mitchell, you got no right." She sat forward with her hands between her knees.

The rain stopped. The clouds shrank away and the wind picked up, drying off the wet boards on the end of the porch. It was ten in the morning.

Mitchell walked out into the yard and watched the last of the clouds sail by as if they were trying to catch up with the others.

He said, "It's like another dawn, ain't it? It's like the day had two dawnings."

And she said, "Yes, Mitchell."

"It's full-blown spring again, ain't it?"

"Mitchell, we ought to start. We don't want to be late. The fires I saw."

He crossed over to her and put a foot up on the porch and a hand on a post. "Okay, we'll start. But, you know, Jenny, Wilson Fellers said I was a good drunk. He said I was happy, not mean like some drunks."

"Mitchell, you're a happy person."

He spent the midday and the afternoon gathering the scrap lumber and burnable debris that had collected on the farm during the past year. There were boards from an old shack he had torn down, limbs and brush that he had cut or the storm had broken; all of it was piled on a hundred-by-nine-foot strip of land that would be used to grow the tobacco plants until they were big enough to be set out singly. He would burn the lumber and trash and the ashes would fertilize the soil and hold off the weeds. It was a good time for it. Most of the wood that was outside had dried by now, but the ground was still wet. The fire wouldn't carry.

Jenny came out to help lift the last of the boards off the wagon. They were long, heavy old oak boards; you couldn't get a nail out of or into them. The work made them both sweat. And then they lit the fire. Henry and the other children threw more scraps into the fire and then began to run around it, chasing each other. It made them all laugh. They all began to gather small sticks lying about and throw them into the fire. It was huge now, burning down its hundred-foot length. The smoke changed directions constantly and they would have to run to avoid it. Still their eyes teared. The fire was leaping into the air and making a big noise. Barn swallows were dashing about, snatching bugs the smoke bewildered. Then Jenny remembered some things she had that were no good and she ran to the house, brought them back and flung them into the fire. Mitchell saw a place that was dying out, so he went to the barn, holding his hat as he ran, and brought back a broken chair and threw it onto the spot. The fire took it instantly. The children were screaming. The smoke was hundreds of feet high. Jenny jumped back and let out a screech when a swallow, in the blue tilt of its wing, seemed to come out of the fire. Then, with a look in his eye, Mitchell hurried to her and said, "It makes you want to take off all your clothes and throw them into the flames, don't it?"

And she said, "Mitchell!"

And he said, "Well, how about just this old shirt? How'd that be?" And he smiled.

18

The Muskatatuck, where the Decatur Road bridge crosses over it at Perry's Store, is narrow but deep. If you had been on your way to Decatur or some other point past Perry's, you probably would chance the shortcut. The shortcut crosses the Muskatatuck at old man Alford's, where the river is wide but shallow and rocky.

I say you might chance the shortcut because you do take a chance. The river may be up too deep to wade. Or, the worse event, you may accidentally run into or get caught by old man Alford. He will start a whole conversation on the pretext of nothing, give him a chance. Sometimes he will follow you right out into the middle of the river, keeping his side of the conversation up. And if he gets you into his little backward shack on the riverbank to show you his collection of feathers and rocks and river junk, you might as well sit down and rest your feet. You won't get out in under two hours.

First thing, he will give you the story of his backward shack. In 1936, when he was sixty-three and the Muskatatuck was flooding, he got an idea. It was clear the water was going to rise up past his shack. So he gathered a bunch of fifty-gallon barrels and tied them together under the house. Then he tied both sides of the house to trees. It almost worked. The river rose and the barrels supported the house. He fished off the front porch for a while. But during the night the upriver cables attached to his house snapped and, unknown to him, the house made a wide arc out into the river and then swung back into the bank. Well, the water receded that night, and when he woke up the next morning and walked out on the porch (it was a bit of a climb and he thought it was just old age), he was looking up into the trees instead of out on the river. So the house has been that way ever since, facing uphill. The floor has about a thirty-degree grade to it. It's all right to lean back in your chair at dinner if you're sitting on the uphill side of the table because that brings you up to level. "So," he says, "I am just waiting on the next flood so I can turn my house back around."

"You want to know why I live on the river?" he will ask. And before you can even shake your head yes or no or maybe, he tells you the word "cycle," and then looks at you for the flash of revelation you're supposed to have on your face. "Don't you see the wonder of this river?" he will say. "It's a little diagram of the way the whole world works." And when he says "little," he will hold his thumb and forefinger about an inch apart, and when he says "whole world," he will spread his arms all the way out. You will think he is talking about the size of a fish.

Then he gets a dark look and you can tell that way back in his head there is a kitchen match striking. "The thin water taken off these ridges and falling into creeks like the Quirks Run will flow to this Muskatatuck, which will be taken into the wider Flint and thence into that awe-river, which I have only seen once, the Mississippi, and thence into the infinite Gulf, which I have never laid eyes on, and from there this same thin water will rise, be pulled and shoved across half the skies of this world, to be finally dropped unconsciously and inscrutably back on these ridges to begin the cycle again and again and again. And the greatness and sadness of it," he will tell you, "the greatness is the thin stream, is that river and the rest, and the ͬadness the raindrops, the drops that you see when you splash the river with a rock. It is more than I can tell you. Break both your legs, it's more than any man can tell you." And while you are wondering how this old man could know a word like "inscrutable," or if he will really break your legs, he will either start crying, or laughing. And if he cries, there will be water streaming down his face. And if he laughs, there will be water on his face. And he will wipe away the tears and say, softly, "See? See?"

19

It was a sunny day. And it was a good thing, because when the delivery van (painted in goldleaf letters: DECATUR RADIO AND PHONOGRAPH—WE DELIVER IN A RADIUS OF 20 MILES) came to a smooth stop on the last few feet of the new gravel stretch on the Decatur Road, Mitchell Parks and his two boys still had nine or ten miles of walking till home, with a load to carry as well. They piled out of the back of the van and Mitchell loaded up the boys with gear and then he gathered up the big box himself. They stood at the side of the road, where the gravel gets thin and mixes with the dirt, and watched the van back up and turn around. It stopped again right next to them and a head with bright-red hair and an even brighter red face popped out at them. It was like a surprise package. "I'm sorry, mister, I'd take you all the way home but the boss checks my mileage. He's got plenty of rules."

"It's all right, Red, me and the boys walk this far all the time. We're practically in the front yard right now."

"Well, don't wear that radio out the first week." And then the van spit a few gravels at them as it headed back down the road to Decatur. The three of them watched it for a long time; then they began to walk. It was like a little safari, Mitchell leading the way with the radio hefted up on one shoulder and four rolls of antenna wire ringing the other arm, Henry behind him with a roll on each shoulder, and Stephen with his roll hanging on his neck, trying to step on his big brother's heels.

Wilson Fellers came by on his mule and said, "Whatcha got?" and then went on. And pretty soon the three of them started to think they were in a movie because all up and down the Decatur Road to home people had gotten word about the new radio and came out on their porches to watch the procession pass. Stephen started to do tricks with his roll of wire, like tossing it up in the air and catching it on his foot. When they came to the bridge over the Muskatatuck there were four or five men in a group waiting on the other side. John Perry saw Mitchell and the little parade first and yelled out, "Look here at Caesar crossing the Rubicon, boys," and they all laughed.

Whip Jordan said, "Mind if I come up and listen sometime, Mitchell? That old radio at Perry's crackles so much, you can't understand a word on it."

John Perry said, "That ain't true." But by that time the safari had passed, and then the men had to hurry to catch up with it.

Whip Jordan said, "You want me to carry the radio for a while, Mitchell? I will." Mitchell gave him the four rolls of wire instead. The rest of the men took some of the wire from the boys, so that everyone had a roll to carry. Stephen gave his up for a nickel. Somehow they all felt obligated to join in at the end of the line, like they were buying tickets to something. The safari was stretched out a good twenty feet. Everyone felt obligated except John Perry, who felt it was his right to walk alongside Mitchell, being the only other radio owner in the area.

"Be glad to show you how to hook that thing up, Mitchell; done mine myself."

"I've got instructions right here, John, no need. Looks like all you got to do is plug it in and hook up the antenna."

"Well, it may sound that easy."

They were passing the old Holland place and the dogs all had their noses stuck through the fence. Holland came out on the porch and watched the safari pass. Some of the dogs quit the fence and ran to him. Mitchell shifted the radio to the other shoulder and looked up at the dog collector. Mysterious fellow, he thought, and was satisfied with that.

The safari was ten members strong now. Two people didn't even have anything to carry. They all kept their eyes stuck on the radio, watched it ride steady and level on Mitchell's shoulder. Even if folks didn't join in, they came out and yelled at Mitchell. Most of them asked if they could come and listen, but old man Webster, who Mitchell thought would never die, came out and said Mitchell wasn't going to get any kind of reception in these hills, called him a young fool, and then kicked at the dirt in the Decatur Road. He was a naturally nasty person.

Whip Jordan said, "What do you think all this antenna wire's for, you old jackass? Mitchell's gonna be able to get Mars if he wants."

Then Webster kicked the dirt in the road again and yelled at his daughter-in-law to come look at this train of fools. She came out on the porch, threw her arms up in the air, seemed surprised when they came back down, and went back inside. The safari went on without them.

But when they'd all made it to the Parks place and stood out in the yard, a thing happened. Mitchell went inside with the radio and before long they heard a big "WHAT?" None of them had figured that Mitchell hadn't told his wife about the radio.

John Perry said, "What in the world has he gone and done?"

Then, real quick, they piled all the wire in the arms of the two boys and started back down the road, taking little quick hops every once in a while to hurry. They stuck their hands in their pockets as they ran, like they had nothing to do with anything on earth. The two boys stood still in the yard. Stephen looked at Henry and said, "I'll give you my nickel if you go in first."

"Honey, it wasn't that much money. What I paid won't keep us from putting a down payment on the farm in a couple of years."

"Still, you should at least have asked me."

"Well, the boys saw it in the window and heard it playing and just had to have it."

"The boys?"

"Well, it seems like if a man works in a coal mine every winter, he ought to be able to listen to a radio in the spring."

"That wasn't fair, Mitchell."

"I know. I know. I was wrong to buy the radio, and it's all I had. It was a kid thing to say."

"I'm glad you bought the radio."

"You want to help set it up?"

"You bought it. You set it up."

In the afternoon Mitchell and the boys stretched the antenna wire to the top of the nearest ridge. At six o'clock the first visitors started to arrive. By seven forty-five the house was full of people. Jenny made three months' worth of coffee in one night. They all sat in a semicircle around the radio. Mitchell didn't even know two of them, and they were the last to leave at one that night. When Mitchell finally crawled into bed beside Jenny he said, "What in the world have I done?"

The people came for two weeks solid, sometimes staying till early in the morning, turning the knobs on the radio, searching for faraway stations. Chicago and Atlanta and New York came in strong late at night. If they stayed up late enough, there were times when they could get foreign countries. Each night Mitchell would go to bed and say, "What in the world have I done?"

Then the kids would fight over it in the day, and want to stay up at night, and one day they broke one of the knobs off and Mitchell had to make up rules.

At least twice a week, after a while, a salesman would show up, having to talk to Mitchell or Jenny for an hour or two. They found out later that Becky had been sending off to all the radio advertisements for free samples. One morning a radio salesman showed up in a musical tie and Mitchell had to threaten him to get him off the place.

But then something happened that topped all the rest. At eleven o'clock one night, after they had had the radio for two months and the visitors and salesmen had slackened off, Holland showed up out in the front yard with one of his dogs. Mitchell had been standing at the window and he watched the old man come into the yard in the light of the half-moon and stand there, as if he didn't know what to do next, or as if he knew, and was just waiting. The man motioned the dog to stand near him when Mitchell came out on the porch.

"What can I do for you, Mr. Holland?"

The man looked at Mitchell and then around the yard. He scratched the dog behind the ears. Then he looked at Mitchell again and said, "Understand you can hear France on your radio."

Mitchell had an impulse to ask him who he had heard it from, since he knew of no one the man spoke to. Instead he said, "Sure can, or at least most of the time. You have to play with the knobs for an hour to get it sometimes."

Holland looked around the yard again and then said, "I'd like to listen." He brought his eyes even with Mitchell's and didn't stir. The moon made faint shadows of the dog and the old man that stretched all the way back into a clump of trees.

"Come in, Mr. Holland."

The man put two fingers on the dog's head and said, "Stay." The dog stretched his two front legs out before himself and laid his head on them, like a tired sphinx.

"You can bring the dog in the house if you'd like. He looks like a good dog." Holland looked at Mitchell with a pair of what Mitchell thought must have been the dullest eyes he had ever seen. The dog jumped up and shook his coat and followed the two men into the house. The man sat in the wicker chair by the window, and the dog, who must have weighed fifty pounds, crawled up in his lap and looked out the window. The man rubbed the dog's throat. Mitchell pulled a chair up close to the radio and turned it on. The lights on the radio came on immediately and the round dial set in the mahogany box looked like a huge, unblinking eye. The set crackled and popped as it warmed up. Jenny came out of the bedroom and asked the man if he wanted some coffee or something to eat, but he simply shook his head and looked out the window.

Mitchell shrugged his shoulders and she went back to bed, leaving the door open.

It was midnight before they could make out the garbled French. Holland hadn't said anything, except to tell Mitchell no, when he asked if he could understand French. Mitchell didn't ask him anything else. They sat there in the front room of the house, Mitchell periodically turning down the volume as the signal got stronger, and the man petting the dog to sleep. Mitchell thought the words were like running water and he would have liked to fall asleep too, but the man sat straight up, as if he were listening closely for one or two key messages. He would cock his head to hear better at times. It reminded Mitchell of the way a dog tilted his head when he didn't understand what you were saying to him.

After four A.M. the signal began to fade, and Mitchell had to turn up the volume, as he had turned it down. At six, when the station was no more than static, the man woke up the dog and went out on the porch. Mitchell followed them out. The gray dawn was gushing through the eastern hills. The dog stretched one back leg and then the other and then urinated on the corner of the porch. The man motioned at the dog and walked out into the yard before he turned to look at Mitchell.

He said, "My first name's Jim, Mr. Parks," flipping it through the air as if it were a shiny coin to Mitchell, who caught it, startled, more surprised that such a man should have a first name than that he should be telling it to him. He almost told Holland his name, but he caught himself. He thought that if he told him he would be ahead of the man again, and he didn't know if the man had anything else to offer. He could have asked him why. He watched Holland and the dog disappear through the trees into the dawn forest.

The air was so fresh that it hurt the skin underneath his fingernails. It made him think of the radio waves moving through the air like the wind, across the whole world, unseen. He couldn't imagine all that electricity, that turmoil, in the air, how that much friction could leave this fresh morning. He had felt in the night some vague possibility, but now it was gone. He turned around in the yard and yawned, and looked at the spot where the dog had urinated. Jenny was at the door. "Why don't you go get some sleep."

He gave her a kiss on the mouth and walked toward the bedroom, yawning and scratching himself. At the door he remembered, and went back and turned off the static on the radio. Then he walked back to the bedroom door, but turned again, and with the physical release of stretching his arms out before him and cocking his head to one side and then the other, he said, "What in the world have I done?"

20

In the land across the river the dawn is a totally different thing. In the knobs, by the time the fog burns off, the sun is high over the ridge. Here, the land is more gently sloping and looks as if God took a razor to it, shaving off all the trees except where he couldn't reach, down in the creek bottoms. The dawn has nothing to hold it back, but comes blatant and stark over the earth's rim. It can cut you in two to look at it.

Coming down the Decatur Road out of the mountains, crossing the bridge over the Muskatatuck, the change is drastic. Instead of trees and rocks and underbrush, there are acres of green calf-high fescue: rabbit cover, cow food, hay in the barn come winter. The change gives you the impression you're going somewhere, that some kind of evolution is happening before your eyes. The road across the river even takes on a new look. It's still just dirt, but it's wide enough for two cars to pass without the outer wheels in a ditch. There are houses as close to each other as a quarter mile. It's all welcome at first. You don't have to walk up and downhill nearly as much. The sunsets spread out for half a planet. The night is vast and full of stars.

But the wind and the clouds, which you can watch come at you from far off, are relentless. There is nothing to stop them. Every act of weather is a total one; when the wind blows, it controls the earth. The cold days go right through you, and the hot days sit on you like some ugly memory. The impression of progress is just that. The long stretches of open road force you to think about the trip, and the thinking lengthens it. The wide road, packed hard as pavement, has no tricks to it. What would have been a sharp turn and a surprise in the knobs is a long, wide arc of a curve, revealing simply more grass, more road. You can see someone walking toward you a mile off, and somehow it's almost an embarrassment finally to say hello when he gets close enough. You've been watching him for the longest time, how he walks and how he holds his head and his hands, and you realize that by the time he's close he knows you as well as you know him. Maybe you can tell him his dawn will be a different thing soon. Maybe he would appreciate that.

21

It was the spring of 1943. The war had been on for a year and a half, and as he glanced down at the wet earth and then at his mud-caked hands he thought that it must be setting time back home, time to pull the tender green tobacco plants out of their beds and set them out. It was a thought he had no time for. Already he was up, his rifle off his shoulder, groping in the darkness for the folds of his parachute. He heard feet splashing behind him in the mud and swung his rifle around. It was Tilman and Captain Price, their chutes bundled up in their arms. They helped him gather up his chute and then all three ran out of the plowed field into the surrounding woods. The dirt among the trees was strewn with granite. They took ten minutes to dig a shallow pit and bury the chutes. There was a spring wind rustling the new leaves in the trees above them. As Captain Price pulled the map out of his pocket, Mitchell squatted down next to him, resting the butt of his gun on his knee. He, of the three men, carried the only rifle. The captain carried a short submachine gun, and Tilman's sole purpose on the mission was to carry the transmitter. It was midnight. They had five and a half hours to make eight miles through the forest without being detected, and then to find the right position along the convoy route. It was a mission of timing.

They went as fast as the woods would permit, jogging across the open spots, trudging through brush, taking half an hour to crawl up the face of a cliff. Mitchell took it all in stride. The captain, four years younger, said to him, "Just like home, huh, Parks?" After three hours their hands and faces were thrashed and bleeding from pushing through the briers in the dark. They found that it was best just to push through whatever was ahead of them. Looking for the clearest path took too much time. When dawn came they were almost too tired to be wary. They reached the ridge above the road that Rommel's convoy would take and scouted along the crest. Down below they could see where the road made a sharp bend around a pond. The trucks would have to slow down there. It was five-thirty.

Tilman set the radio pack up against a tree and cranked it up. It took him several minutes to relay their

79

position, their readiness. The captain paced back and forth, periodically stepping up on a fallen log and trying to look down the fog-covered road below with his field glasses. Mitchell cleaned his gun. There was nothing else to do. He pulled a dark rag out of his back pocket and rubbed down the long barrel. Then he sat with his back to the fallen log, the rifle between his knees. He had looked down at the road behind him through his sights, and decided it wouldn't be a difficult shot. For a moment he wished he had his old gun at home. But this one was good too. A real sharpshooter's piece. There were a few green ferns and mushrooms growing up out of the ground near the log. He reached down and touched them, then pressed the earth around their base. Tilman was smoking a cigarette. The smoke looked like the fog over the valley below them. He hoped it would lift before the convoy came through. "Every man you kill was just about to shoot your brother." That's what they had said in camp.

"What do you think your chances are?" The captain sat down next to him.

"Of killing him? I think I can kill him from here. We don't need to get any closer."

"Good thing. Look."

The fog had lifted somewhat, and down the long valley he could see the headlights flashing in a long chain around a bend. Tilman cranked up the radio and said, "ETA seven minutes." Mitchell watched the string of trucks for a few minutes, then he positioned himself over the log. The convoy swung around the last bend before the pond and began to slow down. There were two open touring cars in front.

The captain, looking through his field glasses, said, "He's in the second car, the back seat." Then he paused. "But there's two back there. I can't tell which one's him. You'll have to get them both."

Just as the cars got within range, Tilman harshly whispered, "Here she comes; she got through." The plane was no more than two hundred feet above the road, banking with the road as it banked. The convoy began to pull off the side of the road. Men scrambled out of the trucks. The first staff car fell into a ditch and rolled over as the fighter plane began to strafe. The second car pulled over to the near side of the road, beneath the ridge. The two officers in the back seat jumped out and hid behind an outcropping of rocks. When the plane had finished its first run it banked up into the blueing dawn, came back around and prepared for another run. The captain tapped Mitchell on the shoulder. As the plane started to fire, Mitchell aimed the rifle and squeezed off two easy rounds. Both officers slumped over. He stuffed the rifle beneath the log. Tilman hid the transmitter under some brush. And then they ran.

There were six miles of the same woods to the coast. No roads, no villages. If they were going to be caught, it would have to be from behind, by foot. It would only take the Germans moments to tell the officers weren't killed by the strafing plane. They would follow. So they ran, stripping their helmets and belts as they ran, plunging, fighting through the underbrush, skidding down hillsides as the sun came up. When they were two miles from the coast they stopped at the top of a small hill and sprawled on the ground panting. They heard the dogs then, and Mitchell said, "Coondogs," before he thought.

The captain asked, "How far?"

Tilman looked at Mitchell. "Maybe a mile and a half." They pushed themselves up from the ground and went on.

They could smell the sea, and feel it, before they could see it. The forest went all the way out to the water. There was a cliff. Tilman went up the shoreline and the captain went down. Mitchell stayed at the spot where they had come out of the forest to relay messages. From far up the coast, after a few moments, he heard Tilman yelling. Mitchell raced after the captain and they both went back to meet Tilman, who had found the rope, tied to a tree and hanging down the cliff. There was a fisherman's dory below. The rope was strong, so they went down it almost on top of one another. The dogs were close now; Mitchell, the last in the boat, said, "Half a mile at most." The sea was calm, silent. Tilman and the captain took the oars and pulled the boat away from the rocks and out into the ocean. Mitchell sat in the back of the boat, one moment looking for the submarine, the other looking back at the coast. He saw the submarine first, rising a hundred yards off the bow. Then he saw the Germans on the coast, the tan dogs stark against the tree line, the gray-uniformed soldiers almost shadows. But he did not mistake the sharp-shooter. He saw him take the extra-long-barreled rifle off his shoulder and pull it around in a wide gleaming arc. And before he could tell Price and Tilman to jump, to swim for it, for God's sake, he heard—the sharp slap of a screen door slamming.

His brothers were fighting; why couldn't he? He had known what they would say, but he made them say it anyway. He walked into the War Office in the Decatur courthouse at the end of the Decatur Road and they told him no, you are a father, you are thirty-six, and you are a farmer; we need you here at home. So there was nothing left to do but walk home that spring and set out the to-bacco. And he was doing it again this year. Doing it now. It was the spring of 1943, and the war had been on for a year and a half. He looked down at the small velvet-leaved plant he was crouching over. It was a faint-heart-ed-looking thing. He poured a cup of water out of a bucket and onto the plant, then pressed the soil firmly around its base. The bag of fertilizer was at one knee. He reached inside and brought out a spoonful of the white grains. He sprinkled them on the ground around the stem.

The screen door slammed, and he was a bit ashamed. Rommel. His art, his lot was to push up dirt around these plants. He turned his head and looked up, sighted down along the long furrow.

22

The Minister Duncan Washer always wears a tie with a little red in it. Before Sunday sermon he always asks his wife, Tilly, if she thinks the tie has too much or not enough color, asks her if she thinks it will "grab" them. She usually just gives him a sly wink. "Tilly," he has to say, "not on Sunday morning." But this always gives him just the little tremor of excitement he needs before climbing behind the pulpit. It gives his voice that occasional pubescent squeak that drives the white-haired ladies in the first pew out of their minds. Each squeak from the minister's blazing-white throat brings a chorus of amens from them, even if he happens to be talking about the church softball team's losing streak (this is one of his most profound doubts, how God's church could have a losing softball team). Not to knock the old ladies: The minister is anything but uncharismatic; his voice and words can crawl right up the back of your leg and spine and make you think there's a spider on your neck.

The New Gospel Church of the Judgment Day sits in a low spot on the Decatur Road about two miles from the Muskatatuck. It is a white box affair with black trim and steeple, with a door cut out of one wall and windows out of the others. There is a gravel parking lot to the side, and out front a little trailer sign that the church rents so the minister can put proverbs out for the sinners and passers-by to ponder. But he doesn't use it much anymore, really only for the times of sermons and meetings. Once, his ire lit by a group of female liberals marching the streets of Decatur in broad daylight, he made up his own little saying. It went: FEMALE EQUALITY IS AN EXPLICIT BIBLICAL PHALLACY. He thought you spelled "fallacy" with a "ph," like "pharaoh." They put it in the paper and everything. That next Sunday almost half of his tie was red.

But that is all over with and forgotten. The war is a big thing now, and religious fervor is at a peak. The minister walks slowly down the center aisle in his narrow-lapeled black suit. His tie has little red polka dots. He climbs up behind the ebony pulpit and you can tell the polka dots have grabbed everybody already. The organ swells and the air is filled with Jesus. One old lady is saying "amen" before he even says a word. A baby cries and the minister stares it down with contempt. The mother mouths an apology. He gives her the wink of an angel. The organ falls away like a curtain being dropped. The minister's Adam's apple moves up and down like a bead on a string. Lord, Lord, the old ladies cry, here he goes. . . .

"First off we want to thank the Lord with a little hand-clapping for our victories in the Philippines last week. I hear it from a good source that we suffered only half as many casualties as the enemy, and while ours were mostly wounded, over nineteen thousand of their men were found to be dead or fast on their way to it. I think we all know, taking nothing away from General MacArthur, that there's only one person to thank. Let's have a little applause. Thank you, thank you. Yes. Now, this really has been a week of good news. We also have learned most recently, folks, to use a phrase from the papers, folks, that the 'Hun is definitely and without doubt on the run.' We must show a little thanks. Clap your hands, folks, you're in His house. Thank you, thank you. Yes. . . ."

23

Despair borne of death. Dusk-worn men walking in the cool stutterings of spring ending, and the woman, dark-scarved, sidesaddle on muleback. Crickets, the first of summer, are screaming in the weeds at the roadside. "Which way to the inn?" She laughs, and the moon, washed out and set on a tabled ridge like a piece of worn china, totters, seems to her to be about to fall, so she leans in the opposite direction to help steady it, and has to catch at the withers stump to stay on the mule. The men stop and help settle her.

"Perhaps we ought to take her back, go back," the old-est says, "she is too weak." But she says no. The men's rusted shovels clank occasionally on the rocks in the road. But how could the owl call his name when he had no name? she wonders. What is this? she wonders. The oldest uses his shovel as a staff, and walks carefully beside the mule in the center of the dirt road. "It doesn't seem fair, I know, not even given a chance, but the Lord giveth. You need to think on the other children, your girls, these two boys." And the two boys, not knowing that they had been forgotten, looked at their mother and felt a strange guilt for their own breathing.

Giveth, taketh awayeth, Lordeth. Indian giver. Anger

boiled out of grief. I am a different person, she thinks. I am not the same person, she thinks. Things are changed with me now. I won't be fooled again. Not even allowed to breathe. This mule walks stiffly. Why cruelty? Why wrath? I won't be fooled again. The bones of this mule are sharp. The woman dark-scarved and the men dun-colored in the dusk, shovels arcing, their loose clothes belted at the waist, trodding party for a burial.

They are five: the oldest, the old man, looser than the rest, father of the mother, wrapped up in old coat and felt hat, worn hand on worn shovel handle, thinking, I am too old for this; why does this have to happen to me when I am old? And the husband, leading the mule with slack cord, and tucked under his other arm, the corpse. Behind the mule the two boys, young men, still smelling the birth in the house, but unable to detect the death. As if so short a life could not have a physical death, but simply returned to where it had come from, to some ethereal place of origin, dissolved and absolved itself and the time it had lived. As if nothing had happened, that this whole day had not existed since the life came into it and left it within a three-hour span, without touching a dawn or dusk. So they were still somehow unsure that the small blue body wrapped in the white quilt and hammered into the small box was their brother. It was this rather: It was the word "birth" and the word "death" inextricably entwined, rending their conception of the two, so that neither existed, or that they were one and the same. They walk behind the mule, their swinging shovels meeting at odd moments, piercing the evening.

The party stops at a hill that rises abruptly from the road. The husband ties the mule to the small gate and sets the small casket, like a cereal box, on a fence post. The woman slides off the mule slowly, walks through the gate and waits. The boys and the old man are already trudging up the hillside. Quickly, the husband, at first torn between the casket and the wife, picks her up and carries her empty body up the hill. He sets her down and rushes back down the hill. Isn't this the strangest thing, he thinks. This is not real. It is dark out tonight, he thinks. The moon, bleached, has risen, and the crickets chirp in full confusion. The grass is full of them. What has happened to the frogs this year? The casket is light. Again, he tucks it carefully under his arm, and moves up the hill. The bleached moon glances off the tombstones and leaves faint shadows on the dead leaves lying in the graveyard. The farthest reaches of the yard are dark, taken over by poplar and papaw stands. Cattle can get in the graveyard there, he thinks. He places the box on a well-kept grave. The woman and the old man have taken seats next to where the boys have begun to dig.

But it is not even that, she thinks. Thinking, it is not even the attention of cruelty or wrath. It is worse than that. It's some kind of complete indifference. As if we were a dirty rag in the corner he doesn't want to pick up. He is less than human, less even than us. This marker is cold. I won't cry again. I won't be fooled again.

The shovels, dirt-burnished, gleaming as they writhe out of the grave. The boys sweating, but moving, working steadily, not fast but to a beat. "If you stop, your backs will ache. Don't stop. Just keep up a rhythm," the man says, and walks around and around the hole.

She thinking, then it's hopeless. Nothing matters one way or the other. If a baby can be born and die within one morning, nothing matters. I will not cry again. I won't be fooled again. Crying is no different from laughing. I might as well have killed the child myself. Well, I won't be fooled.

"Okay," the man says, and helps the boys out of the hole, ten times the size needed. He takes a shovel and squares off the corners of the grave, scrapes out a few half-shovels of loose dirt. He picks up the small casket and climbs down into the hole. And out of this sight, barbaric and immutable, the grief returns to her. All weight and pervasiveness, dust-ridden and old, all hope distilled and crushed into her throat and skull.

"Maybe we made a mistake," she screams, "maybe it can breathe now, maybe it will breathe now."

She rises, but her knees give and she sits back down. The old man holds her. Her mouth is empty of air. The husband climbs out of the hole and the boys wait till he says, "Give me the shovel," before moving. He buries his son.

The old man says, "We ought to say something, we ought to say something, at least." But the man continues, his heavy breathing following each stroke into the mound of dirt. He finishes, but the dirt that came out of the hole is more than can be put back into it. A small mound rises above the lay of the land.

She stands up and says, "It's just not fair, goddammit. He didn't even get a chance." So the husband takes her and she says not to him and not to the others, not to herself but to no one, "No, no, no, I care, goddammit, and it's like he's going to be with me always; like I'll never have to give him up or let him go away, and I'm going to cry forever, whenever I want to and . . ." And she submerges, her eyes bleached, into the man's clothes, and he carries her back down the hill.

And as she cries he understands the truth of it, not the reasoning but the truth of it, in what she said, for through him like some strange bolt of innocence passes the most welcome but unexplainable bit of envy. And he sees again, Mitchell does, as he carries her to the mule's back, the morning twelve hours past. The surprisingly easy birth for a thirty-six-year-old woman, the unsmiling doctor, then her face, and then the memory of his own face becoming rigid and drawn. They had known, known minutes after the birth that the death would follow. Jenny had said, "Give him to me," opened her shirt and lain the child there, each of his laboring breaths shuddering through her breastbone and on through her. There was, for the three hours, only her duty to keep him warm.

24

The summer wanders in out of the spring sighing, and settles itself like dust motes in the afternoon sun. It folds its arms, looks grudgingly up the Decatur Road, then down it, and then finds a grassy spot on the roadside and sits there amid its own dust, chaff, and seed of the world, sits there brooding, all torpor and heat and humidity, drowsing.

You know the long summer has begun. You are walking along and a glistening sweat comes to your forehead. Wipe that off. The Decatur Road has been graveled as far as twenty miles out, and you are walking on that now. The gravel is of every different kind: creek stone, crushed granite and quartz, cement chips. It puts up a gray dust that sticks to your socks and cuffs. It is hot. You put, maybe, three gravels in your mouth and suck on them. It keeps your mouth wet, but God, the dirt on them goes down dry at first. Here is a billboard: CRYSTAL CAVERNS —SEE THE BLIND BATS—247 MI. The country and the road far behind you, and farther ahead is still grass and tree-lined creek bottoms, houses and barns here and there. Sleepy stuff. So you develop a shuffle, a gait, and let your body do the walking, three-part: The hip swings the thigh out to about thirty degrees, the knee snaps to with the centrifugal force, and the shin lines up with the thigh when the foot is a thousandth of an inch above the earth.

Swing, snap, step. There are plenty of things to do once the walking is taken care of. You've got your hands to contend with. Put them in your pockets, maybe. Get you some gravels and pitch at the sparrows strung on the barbed-wire fences that line the road. You know you'd feel awful if you were to hit some poor bird, but you trust your bad aim. The thing is not to let loose side-arm or something. Side-arm's got too much luck with it. Throw one side-arm in a thousand and you'll kill a sparrow dead-over. Here comes a truck. It's yellow. The driver rolls out a "helloooo" and then the truck is gone. A hubcap was missing. Nice truck, though. Maybe you'll find that hubcap. HISTORICAL MARKER 1/4 MILE. It seems like an awful early warning for a person walking. Your mind is filled with a yearning for that historical marker. Lord, the possibilities. The gravel is spread out in a half-moon before it. *On this spot in 1863 Colonel Perry Milton Morgan was killed while defending the southern embankment of the Decatur Road.* "Well," you say out loud, since the occasion seems to call for it. Then you see a pop bottle down in the ditch, probably right where the colonel became a historical marker, and you go down and put that in your back pocket, neck first. Nickel for it. A little farther on, maybe, you see a good solid stick. Put that in your palm and walk with it. If you've got a pocket knife, you carve as you walk; yes, put your mark on it.

There is more sweat on your forehead now. There is a big nice tree to the side, so you decide to sit there under it. Well, it is summer. Between your breath and your outstretched legs you see a rock, some lone gravel spit from the road by a hoof or a tire. The rock has a fossil in it, impression of some nameless creature that moved over the earth millions of years ago. Maybe there is a little speck of blue quartz in the rock, too. Pick that up. Well, it is certainly a long day's walk to Decatur. You have got that much figured out.

25

It was early summer, June again, for her the cruelest month, bringing memory and desire, that already-old burden only two years past. But it was just the time of the year. This would pass. It had been a week since the birth/death day; she had offered her presence and given herself up to the memory for a time and now she felt herself slipping back to the present. There was a sadness in this passing too, almost a guilty sadness, but it was something, she realized, that had to be done. And besides, it was June, the evening, and Henry was leaving. Dinner had to be ready soon. He would be voraciously hungry. "Voracious"—what a word, she thought.

She strained the water out of the green beans, then gave the pot to Becky to put on the table. The potatoes were ready too, so she brought them to the sink, poured out the hot water, and began to mash them with a big fork. Just outside the window over the sink she could see the robin in its nest. The bush under the window had become very thick this spring, the robins had chosen it as a home, and she had watched them for weeks at mealtimes: bursting out of the bush's foliage and returning with a twig or a piece of dry grass; the male robin somewhat of a scavenger, bringing back strings of burlap, small pieces of paper, and once the tag from a pair of her underwear. It must have fallen to the ground when she hung out the wash. When the nest had been strengthened and the basic shape made, the little male bird would get involved in the most horrible fights, sometimes carrying home to the female a bright feather plucked from another bird to soften the nest, other times coming home absolutely beat-up. Then, two weeks before the eggs came, the female had plucked down from her own breast to line the nest. She sat on the eggs now. They would hatch soon. "Here, Becky, put these in a bowl." She gave Becky the potatoes and then took the lid off the frying chicken. She turned it once or twice, took a piece or two out, and then put the lid back on. The robin had its head tucked under a wing.

"Momma, are you going to make gravy? You know I think Henry's got his heart set on a miracle happening to him. I sure hope it does. He's too stupid to make it otherwise."

"He is not. He's a smart boy. He'll do good in the army. What did you say? I mean you said something else."

"I said Henry was stupid."

"No, the first thing you said, something about me."

"Oh, I asked if you were going to make gravy."

"Oh."

"Well?"

"I guess so. I don't know."

"You drive me crazy sometimes, Momma."

She took the chicken out of the pan and told Becky to go call her brothers and sister. "Your father's out in the barn." She poured some of the grease in the pan into an old coffee can. It was an orange can, and she put it back up on the windowsill. The skillet was heavy; it took both hands to carry it back to the stove. She shook some flour into the remaining grease, poured in a glass of milk, then added salt and pepper and stirred. The gravy steamed and thickened. She had to put her elbows against her stomach to brace her forearms when she lifted the cast-iron pan from the stove and tilted it over a bowl. It took a long time for the gravy to pour out. As the pan got lighter she was able to get a spoon and scrape out the bits of chicken crust. She put the pan in the sink, the bowl on the table, and checked on the robin one last time. "All right, where is everybody? This stuff'll get cold. I'm gonna eat."

The room filled with people sliding chairs and grabbing at the chicken plate.

"Where's Henry, Stephen?"

"He ain't gonna eat. Says he ain't hungry. Keeps packing and packing his stuff in Uncle Brice's duffel bag."

They filled their plates. Stephen put down a piece of bread and spread gravy over it. Sarah, the youngest, put gravy on everything.

Becky said, "Sarah, don't put gravy on your green beans, for goodness' sake."

"I'm thirteen and shall do whatever I please, thank you. Momma, I like gravy."

Becky speared a green bean. "You're gonna be fat as a pig, you little snot."

Mitchell said, "Becky, nobody in this house ever said you was going to be fat. You don't say it."

She laid down her fork and almost cried.

Jenny called, "Henry, come in here and eat right now."

"I ain't hungry. Ain't got the time."

Mitchell said, "Let him go. He'll get something before he leaves. Y'all leave some for your brother."

Jenny got up from the table and put three pieces of chicken in a towel and laid it on the counter. This is a big day in my life, she thought. I hope three pieces are enough. And she went back to the table and began to eat.

"Mother," he had said, sitting in the living room next to the new gas stove, barefaced, in a white T-shirt, "I am idle here. Dad and Steve don't need me. With this stove and the gas, I don't even need to cut wood anymore. These hills can only support a few men. There ain't no profit; I'll get out of school and not be good for anything but sleeping and eating. I don't hate this place, but I've got to go. Out there are whole cities of people, all of them different,

93

all over the world. And it all just seems to gleam before me, and . . ."

And she had said, "It's all the same as here, I know it; you'll go one place and have to go to another. Everything just moves backward before you."

"But, Mom, it's so dull here. I feel like I'm rusting through, or washing away a little bit at a time down that creek. It seems like all we do here is breathe, and that isn't enough. I just want to see all that out there. Once."

"Your father wants you to stay."

"I know he does. I can't. This is his country. I feel like it's some kind of island. But he belongs here and I love him here. He does good and useful things. But he works his work, and I want to work mine." He had said these things.

Her beans were cold. Outside a 1934 Chevrolet pulled up and honked. It was Matt Hallam, come to pick up her boy. Henry stumbled out of his room and everyone got up from the table.

Mitchell said, "You leaving already? Jenny, get him something to eat."

"Here," she said, "come on and eat."

"I can't; Matt's waiting."

She went to the counter and gave him the bundle of chicken. They all walked out on the porch. The long June day waning; the slow moon climbing. The car's headlights shot out through the evening. Matt got out of the car and shook hands with Mitchell, then put Henry's bag in the back seat of the car.

"I thought that I'd never get to go. But it's not too late I don't think. I'm on my way," Henry said.

"You're only eighteen," Mitchell said. "Shut up."

Matt said, "Some work of noble note may yet be done, not unbecoming men, say, Henry?"

"Right. You see, our purpose is to sail beyond the sunset."

94

"You boys be careful," she said.

"We will, ma'am."

Henry hugged them all and then the boys left. She walked back in the house, cleared the table. She watched the bird, as well as she could in the dark, as she washed the dishes. Then she walked out on the porch and sat with Mitchell, who hadn't been back in the house yet. "It was the food," she said, "we let him eat too much."

26

In the evening, especially during the languor of the long summer months, it was her pleasure, Miss Green's, to sit on the veranda of her small frame house. It was a neat house, and the porch swing hung straight and true, and only squeaked on the back swing. The yard was smooth and green, but it was a yearly battle for her to cut back the creepers it sent out across her narrow sidewalk. The sidewalk ran like an arrow between two large, perfectly symmetric maples, all the way out to the Decatur Road.

She would make herself a cup of tea, with sugar and cream, sometimes with a slice of orange or lemon; this would make her feel strangely exotic, since most people drank coffee; it would make her feel almost criminal—the steam, the brilliant odor, the piquant taste, the brittle china cup. She would make the tea, then walk slowly down the short hall in her slippers and stop in the small, dour, but quaint front room to pick out a novel. The books were all gilt-edged and lettered, leather-bound, and pressed tightly side-to-side in heavy, glass-shuttered book-cases. On top of the bookcases were many portraits, some old and faded, framed in oval gold-enameled frames, some portraits newer, with silver and wood frames. There were also many trinkets lining the tops of the shelves and the mantel of the little fireplace—china and pewter and brass, tiny carved figurines, all gifts. She liked to pause and look at them. The room was a tad dark, so she usually selected four or five likely titles, stacked them and placed her teacup on top. Then she tottered with the whole bunch across the faded but clean oriental carpet to the hallway and then to the porch. At times the screen door would present a problem. Its spring was very tight, and she was constantly being slapped on her behind. She reminded herself to ask one of her men friends to mend it. Out on the porch she placed the books on the swing, fingered through them the way the wind might, and finally chose one. She loved her books dearly, and occasionally wrote tightly structured, precise reviews for the Decatur *Advocate-Messenger*. She was glad when her reading carried her far off and faraway, she liked Joseph Conrad and Henry James best, but she was just as glad to come back home after reading them, to her neat house and yard, to the maples and the world passing by her on the Decatur Road. But she did not feel as if the world were passing her by; it was more like all the world came to her, slowed in its walking to glance or chat, left its best part, and then went on. Many times the glance or chat turned into something more, and these instances, along with her evenings in the squeaking swing, made life bearable for her, made it endurable and happy. It was the combination or mixture of the two, her private world and the moments the outside world came into it, that gave her opportunities to understand the evil and the sadness that had been hers during, what she thought was, such a long, long life.

She took a sip of tea, and brought her legs up beside her in the swing. The evening was full of coolness and shadow. There were lightning bugs sporting under the maples and as far out as she could detect them. Her book was about the Far East, about a solitary man in white among the dark natives. She gave her heart to him for a moment and then withdrew it, decided it was hers best to keep. She was still very young. Oh, the night was cool, and moved silkily inside her housecoat. She could see the first stars coming out and the moon already high in the blue, blue night. She could dimly make out the creepers moving out across the sidewalk. And down the evening-covered Decatur Road, down the long road at the crest of a small hill, under cover of darkness, followed by some somber tail-dragging dog, came her first customer. She put aside, for this moment, her precious book.

27

"Do not forsake me, oh, my darling!"

"Please, Daddy, hush, the march is about to start. Be serious just this once. Now, don't step on my dress. Is everybody sitting down yet?"

"You know, honey, you used to sleep between me and your Momma. You don't have to go through with this if you don't want to."

"Daddy, please be serious. And make sure you keep in step with me when the march starts. You won't fall, will you? I'll die before this is over, I'll die."

"Well, you want to talk about something while we're walking? We should probably lean over to one another and whisper while we walk. Make everybody think we're saying real important sentimental stuff. Course we can talk about anything. You know, the communists or something."

"Daddy, you're gonna make me cry. I think I'll cry anyway."

"If it'll give you something to do."

"Oh, God! It's started. Okay, you open the door and let me step out on the porch and then you join me. Then we'll step, in time, to the march. You won't mess up, will you? I'll die if you mess up. Okay, go ahead."

"Geronimo!"

"Daddy!"

He couldn't decide whether to shut the door behind them or join Becky. Probably best to leave it open. Flies would get in the house but that could be dealt with later. He took her arm.

The organ, belligerent and proud through the wedding march, was to their immediate left on the porch. Mrs. Thumson looked up from her playing and smiled brightly at Mitchell, as if they shared some humorous secret that no one else in the wedding party had the least notion of. Mitchell smiled back at her because she had a little piece of black olive stuck to a front tooth. Here was the secret, he thought. How nice of her to share it with him. She was a saint. But he was father of the bride. Father of generations. The ol' species gets another kick in the pants today, he thought. Becky gave him a gentle tug, and they took their first step. Like Astaire and Rogers, Rooney and Garland, the Scarecrow and Dorothy. I could dance all the way up the aisle. These porch steps are worn on the edge. Put new ones on before long. What do you do with the old ones? Lots of footprints on these steps. These shoes hurt. Push that third toe up; it ain't got no room. Toenail's cutting the sock; thin little ol' silk sock anyway. Maybe I could hop on the other foot and save the sock. Better not.

There, the grass is better. Looks good. Worth fencing it off to keep the goats out. Must be a hundred and fifty goats here. They're all dressed up nice. Pretty bunch of people. Blue skies and just a breeze, man, man. Best day this year, bar none. Would you look at all these folks turning to look at us. Ought to run my finger up my nose or something spectacular like that. There's a June bug. Wonder how he's made it this far without being squashed. Shouldn't have looked down. Lord God, hope I don't trip. Just don't look down again. Just step to the march. How long is this thing gonna last? Flies are gonna control the house in a few more minutes. Lunch ain't no treat waving at flies the whole time. Should have shut that door. There is, I have just realized it, a stupid-looking smile on my face. Need to get that off. Don't want to smile, but there it is anyway. Work on that bottom lip first. Impossible. Now the inside crook of my elbow is sweating. Will this hell never cease? Okay, stop here for a minute while Mrs. Thumson pumps up the organ for another go. Piece of black olive.

They stop just before the last row of folding chairs. There is a length of red carpet rolled out before them leading up to a homemade altar. It is painted a brilliant white. The preacher stands behind it, smiling. Everybody is smiling. All of the people, sitting in the folding chairs, look at the father and the bride. The preacher, dressed in white, gives a little nonchalant signal.

I wonder if I could beat that fellow in white on the draw. Better not try it. Some innocent bystander might get injured.

The music opens up again and they begin to walk down the red-carpeted aisle. As they pass, the rows of people turn around all at once like the Rockettes and watch them pass.

I am the father of generations and this is my daughter Nokomis, daughter of the Moon. We are links in the great chain and we hold, bear our tension. She is better than I, part of her mother; she is the daughter of generations and to be the mother of thousands. There is a spider on John Perry's shoulder. Can't stop to slap at it now. Guess he'll get it when it reaches his neck. First Methodist Church: They did that with a stencil on the back of every one of them chairs. Who'd steal a church's chair? We are almost there. This is the longest walk I have ever took. Baptist preacher in a white suit. He's got him a yellow flower on

99

his coat. Oughta get me one of them. Got no hair on his head, though. Baptist preacher, Methodist chairs. There is Wilson Fellers standing over the punch bowl. Baptist preacher, Methodist chairs, Catholic punch. Why, somebody's not here; there's an empty seat up front. That's a good seat too, somebody ought to have gotten that one. You can still smell that dead fish under the house. Gonna kill that cat. There's ol' man Alford. Must be eighty if he's a day. Ain't got a tooth in his head, but you can tell he's smiling by the way he squints. This is like running the gauntlet. No telling when the folks on both sides are going to pull out their clubs and axes. We are almost there. Honor thy father. She has deceived her father and may thee. Father of generations. Father not of countries nor waters nor modern medicine but of my family. And this, my daughter, at my side. Carrier of the blood of generations. She, humanity's most perfect. The preacher smiles. Everyone is smiling. I must be happy, I am smiling. Must stand still. The music is over. Who is tugging on my trousers? It's Jenny.

"Daddy, you can sit down now," Becky says.

"What? Oh." What is going on here?

He sits. He looks up at her.

But he had waited! Hadn't he waited, and now here she was marrying someone else?

28

Seventeen miles outside of town on the Decatur Road there is an old house surrounded by vast, windy porches, turned wood, baroque trim, maples with heads like balls of wire, high grass. It is an old house, full of old births and deaths, old stains—blood and water and coffee—stuffed with wallpaper seven layers thick, newspapers under that (accounts of a double murder and an old surprise), and under the house itself old bones, old broken toys, a tarnished spoon. The driveway, from the Decatur Road to the house, has blended into the fields.

This, they thought, would be their new home. It would take, they thought, a little work. They pulled up in front in the car, making a path through the tall weeds. The woman carried in a broom and a dust pan, and the man carried in a wooden box of tools.

They were newlyweds, married just a few weeks. The young man had wanted to rent an apartment in Decatur, but the girl said she needed to be closer to her parents, who lived in the hills. So they made a down payment on the old house. Besides, she had said, their money wouldn't be just going down the drain, they would own their own home. It would be permanent, instead of month-to-month.

They had to break a pane of glass to get in the house. The key hadn't been right, or the lock was jammed. They set to work immediately. They scraped peeling paint, threw out trash, and swept until the house breathed in air and exhaled dust. They had to move outside themselves periodically to get some fresh air. It seemed that the more they scraped and swept, the more there was to be scraped and swept. The floor in the kitchen and the entranceways was rotten, and she swept through half an inch of wood before she realized what she was doing. She scraped on the banister, but only half of the old paint would come up. If they painted over it, there would be lumps. She reached up into a corner with her broom to pull down a spiderweb and she knocked a hole in the ceiling. The plaster came down wet and mildewed. For some reason there were, it seemed, whole bales of hay between the walls and between the floors and ceilings. "Birds and rats," her husband said, and smiled. He was very happy, hammering and tearing out boards, finding old junk in closets and attics. He showed her an old shoe and a bottle. "Isn't this wonderful," he said. His face was covered with dust. "You were right for us to do this," he said.

They worked all morning and afternoon. Toward the evening she went upstairs and crawled into the attic to find him. She said, "Why don't we get cleaned up and go to Momma's and Daddy's for dinner?" She was tired.

"We've eaten there for three weeks in a row, honey. Let's stay in the house tonight. It's our first night."

She went back downstairs and walked from room to room. There was more to pick up now than when they had gotten there that morning. She tripped over an old board and finally found a place to sit in the back room. She couldn't get the thought out of her mind that her mother was starting dinner at home and it was just a few miles down the road. She couldn't get used to just cooking for two. When she had helped her mother cook, they made big pots of everything. She heard her husband hammering on something in the attic. It was a lonely, faraway sound, like the beating of her heart. Her nose was full of dust, and her face, no matter how many times she wiped it, felt as if it were covered with strands of cobwebs. And then, realizing she would have to make something for herself and him to eat, and later make some sort of bed for them, she thought that the daughter and sister in her had just been killed, felt that she was another old ghost in this haunted house, that the road home, that old umbilical, had finally snapped. And this house, the walls of this house, stuffed and portentous and stained, would have to be stripped and washed down with a hose before she could be born again, born wife, born mother.

29

Fooled by a sun that burned forever, never set, a few
spastic dust-covered moths fluttered around a bare bulb
that lighted the train-station platform. A dirty, wrinkled
string hung down from the bulb's base. The 4:45 A.M. to
Lexington was long out of sight, but Mitchell and Jenny
still lingered on the platform. It was the morning of the
summer solstice and their youngest, the last child, had just
left for summer work and college in the fall. They sat
down on a wrought-iron bench that had been painted a
hundred times with white paint. The train had taken its
size and noise and left a great empty space. The station
seemed much smaller and simpler now. There was the
platform with the bare bulb, the long stretch of the tracks
that came from and went who knows where, and inside,
the open room with chairs, the ticket window, and the
small diner. The little station was too far outside of town
to gather size and strength from surrounding buildings.
Here there was only an open field. It was still dark out, the
meadowlarks still hadn't risen, and the stars were like
bulbs far up in the sky, without the dangling string. The
rest of the morning, till dawn, seemed fairly useless to
them. There was only the time to be gotten through, and
the station, cold and distant, like a drop of dew in the
grass, was as good a place as any to keep pace with the
dark morning's slow time to dawn. It was just now five
o'clock.

He looked out across the open fields and said to her, "I
think we ought to take vacations now. I was reading about

it in a magazine inside. People take a week or two weeks out of the year, jump in the car, and go across the country looking at things. We might go see the Grand Canyon and Niagara Falls."

"You gave her the extra money?"

"Yes."

Far down the line, through the night, they heard the whistle as the train went through the outskirts of Decatur. A porter, his clothes wrinkled from the naps he had taken between incoming trains, came out on the platform and gathered up towels the Pullman cars had left.

"You folks miss the train? Won't be no other in here for forty-five minutes. Might catch you a snack in the diner. Long wait on a cool morning. Get in there now and beat the crowd. Food hot now. Can't allow you to be out on the platform between trains. I almost didn't get the clean towels back on that train. Did you see? Would have got fired for that. Rush, rush, rush. Can't hardly keep up with it. It's a clean tip. Food's hot now. Beat the crowd. Better wash your hands first; bathroom's right over there; that woman in the diner's a she-devil when it comes to keeping it clean."

"Why don't we eat before going home?"

"All right."

It was as if a big weight had been taken off their laps. This was something that required action. They walked back through the lobby where a young boy in uniform read a magazine and an old man slept, stretched across four chairs. The man behind the ticket window was writing on slips of paper. The diner was along one wall, enclosed in glass. There was a long bar with eight or nine stools, and booths were next to the glass partition that opened on the lobby. The stools and booths were all covered in bright-red vinyl and trimmed with chrome armrests and legs. There were neon signs in all the windows, bright red: NINA'S DINER   24 HOURS   CAMEL

CIGARETTES. The bar and all the trash cans were stainless steel and brightly polished. Behind the bar, between the ventilation hoods, were spotless mirrors. The whole place shone. Even the floors, black-and-white checkerboard, glistened. It was breathtaking.

They sat in a booth and wondered how food could be served in such a place. They took menus, printed on some kind of silver paper, out of a little chrome stand that also held glass salt and pepper shakers (chrome tops). There was only one other person in the diner. She was standing next to the chrome cash register counting stacks of dimes. She had a towel over each shoulder.

"Be with you folks in a jiff," she jingled, then she took a handful of the dimes to the jukebox and punched buttons as if the machine were a typewriter. "Nothing like pop to wind up the last two hours of a shift, whatchasay?" Soon the glass-box diner was vibrating with the music. The waitress, in a white dress that barely covered her knees, fairly hopped, skipped, and jumped to their table. There were more cleaning towels stuffed around her belt and hanging out of her pockets. "You folks will want coffee. I'll get it on the count of point five." And she was off, a flurry of cleaning rags, a human feather duster. Then she was back.

Mitchell said, "I'd like a couple eggs over-easy, some bacon, and some toast."

"You order by the number here, kid," she said. "See, look here, we got everything numbered on the menu, up to twenty-five. You gotta order a number. Which number you want? See, I gotta put the numbers down in the books for the boss from now on so it's easy to track. Some neon brain's been taking from the till and he had these menus made up. Order by the number."

"I'll have a number three," he said.

"Apprecio mucho."

And Jenny said, "Me too, but I only want one egg."

"What number is that? Give me a number. Words do me no good. We ain't allowed to turn words into numbers. I can suggest you look at number twenty-two and see if that's what you want, but I can't listen to words and write numbers."

"Yes," she said, "I'll have a number twenty-two."

"A three and a twenty-two, very good. Oh, honey, you've got a crack in your coffee cup. Can't serve you in that. Against the law. Get you another."

Jenny looked up at Mitchell after she had gone and said, "I think I ought to punch her; what do you think?"

The two numbers came soon, and they ate their breakfast with an automatic motion of elbow and wrist, bringing food to their mouths as if they were the jukebox's mechanical arm lifting on a new record. Mitchell ate a piece of bacon and said, "That was the last of them; she is a good fifteen miles on her way by now, I'd say."

"Yes, they're all gone."

"Do you suppose we will get fat now?"

"Not playing in your food like you are. I don't think I want to go back to the big house."

"It's a little house."

"It's a big house."

"We got to go back sometime. But I don't feel much like moving from this spot myself. Feel like just sitting here."

"It's like having a baby. This is what it's like."

They watched the people coming into the lobby beyond the glass partition: a young man in a dark-blue suit carrying absolutely nothing; an old couple, the man all in white, the woman all in black; an odd-looking boy, who seemed to have the wrong head on his shoulders. The whole world was awry. The old man who had been sleeping woke up when the man behind the ticket window yelled, "Line up for the five forty-five." He unfolded his coat and rubbed his red, creased cheek. The train pulled in, and all the people in the lobby went out on the

106

platform and boarded. It was still dark outside. The diner had never had a crowd to beat. Perhaps it would come later. They slid out of the booth and left the waitress a dime.

"Everything a shine?" she asked.

The lobby was deserted again. No one had gotten off the 5:45. The sleeping man had left a newspaper and the boy in uniform had left his magazine and an ashtray full of butts. The lobby seemed thousands of years older than the diner. There was dust and smoke in the air and the tile floor was worn in front of each chair. The ticket agent broke the dead air when he shouted, "Christ, why don't they drop the goddamn bomb on the whole country and forget it!" He was reading a newspaper. He must have thought the station was completely empty. They stopped before the door to the parking lot. There was a gumball machine with a little sign on top: *The Lions Club thanks the L&N line for donating the space this machine occupies.*

"Want a gumball?"

"Okay."

Mitchell put a penny in and two black balls rolled out. "You hate licorice, don't you? Me too." He put in another penny and a yellow and a green came out. He gave Jenny her choice. The waitress in the diner picked up her dime tip and waved at them and mouthed a silent "thanks for nothing." A bronze earth with "North," "South," "East," and "West" stamped on it was embedded in the floor in front of the doors. Mitchell looked down at the arrows and then looked up.

"This is off a little," he said. She laughed at him, and they went outside.

The sky was a light white to the east. They could feel the warmth returning to the air. Across the road a meadowlark skimmed low across an empty field. Up above them the weather vane on the train station gave an awful squeak and swung heavily around to the west. As they

walked toward their truck they could hear the 5:45 pulling out, and stopped a moment to watch it.

"They go like that all day long," he said. Their black
pickup truck was covered with the morning dew. Jenny
got in and Mitchell turned on the motor. There was a big
empty space on the seat between them, so Jenny moved
over next to Mitchell, put her hip next to his. She had seen
young people do this. It was her first chance.

"It has been such a short time since they came. We
should talk about them, the kids."

"I'm sure we will."

"I mean to other people, not just ourselves," Jenny said.

"No. It was one of my biggest surprises, finding out that
our kids are just like everybody else's. Our kids are everybody's kids."

"Well, I don't believe that."

"Me neither."

The sun, three quarters above the mountain horizon,
sparkled through the dewdrops on the windshield. Mitchell turned on the wipers and the world lay suddenly clear
all before them. They were, they realized, alone together.
The sun lifted itself onto the flat of the mountains and
seemed to stand still, to stop, as if it would burn there
forever, before moving on. It was the beginning of the
longest day.

30

He was spawn of that old joke: His father sold himself to
his mother, an Oklahoma reservation Cherokee, but went
as he came, leaving the seed of a son in her, a free sample.
His father, that old Indian giver. He was a pink color, she

told her son, a New Yorker selling novelty items. She told her son this, left him with this legacy, then died. He, the son, packed his things, his wood-carving tools, his clothes, and left the reservation with his mutt dog. He headed for New York but wound up in middle ground, wandered down the Decatur Road, saw an opportunity. He would, he decided, let his father pass. He sold what he had and bought a gas pump and two tanks, one for regular and one for ethyl. Halfway down the road he bought a quarter acre, dug a deep hole, buried his two tanks and set the dual pump above them. He put out a sign: JAMES T. FEATHERS—GAS. He and the dog sat on a flat rock.

He sold gas, fueled the goings of others, and in the meantime he gathered fine wood for his carving. In a year he bought back the tools he had sold and built himself a two-room block building. One room he and the mutt slept in and ran the gas station out of; the other was his wood shop. The Coca-Cola Company put a machine out front. The farmers came to buy a Coke or gas and would sometimes stay to watch him carve in his shop. He would fashion their faces in a piece of cherry. A chain out of a stick would take only half an hour. Soon, word got back to Decatur. Women would force their husbands to drive the sixteen miles out of town for gas so they could see the mestizo carver. He created scenes on the wooden arms of their best chairs. He carved the nativity on a parson's tabletop. He put the feet and claws of a monster on the legs of the most harmless of piano stools. He carved his wood and sold gas.

Then, in the summer of 1937, when he had been at his station and carving for six years, a woman from Lexington came and asked him to make the frame for a painting. She gave him a picture of the painting and its dimensions. He looked at the picture and smiled and said okay. The frame took eight weeks. He threw away two early versions. The woman came and said she loved it. A few weeks later

109

another woman came, a woman from a New York museum, and she asked him for a frame also. She gave him a sheet of paper that said he had been "commissioned" to do the work. She gave him the dimensions of a painting but did not have a copy of the painting. He said he would not be commissioned unless he got a picture. It came in the mail a week later.

The painting was of angels and babies resting on clouds, and he thought that it was a very sad thing, they all seemed very heavy on the flat paper, to be such light creatures. He took an afternoon away from the station and went into the hills to find the perfect piece of wood. He would carve his frame from wood taken off as high a place as he could find. The wood would be light and full of air. There would be wind in it. He found his stock and brought it off the mountain. He held it in his hands for hours at a time, he let it cure for months, before he put his knife to it, running his thumb along the grain, placing it next to his nose and sighting down its length. He looked at the painting again, setting it next to the wood. He would, he decided, bring the angels and the babies out of the heaviness and flatness of the picture. They would rise slowly from the canvas to the frame's edge until their delicacy and form and demeanor were returned to them. He sharpened his tools, he swept out the shop, he walked around the little block building once or twice, then he began. He worked for six months, buoying the figures in the two-inch thickness of wood. He finished, packed it up in a crate with a note saying that he would like to do another. The pictures and the dimensions came regularly. The woman said she was quite pleased. His frames complemented the masterpieces nicely. The museum was very grateful.

He made twenty frames in the next fifteen years, all of them sent to hang in the New York museum. Each frame was almost a year out of his life. He continued the painting's theme onto the frame; he made little jokes in the wood when he thought a painting was silly. He married a homely woman, and winked at her during the day, for no special reason at all. They raised children. He decided to go to New York and see his work.

He and his wife, a bit haggard and afraid, walked up the worn marble steps of the museum and into a large columned room. A young girl took their entrance fee. Paintings hung all along the walls of the large open room. It was very quiet. James T. Feathers walked slowly with his wife from one painting to the next, reading the names of the artists. He was very proud. He found the first frame he had done for the museum. The wood had not split. His wife asked, "But where is your name, James T. Feathers?" And he did not know what to say. It was very unfair, he knew. But he watched the other visitors, hushed and awed, point at the paintings and say, "Yes, yes." He would, he decided, let this pass too.

31

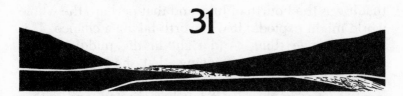

They were sitting on the front porch when he first said it. The most ordinary place in the world. The wind was blowing gently across them and a pretty song was on the radio. Mitchell was snapping his fingers, tiny explosions to the music. Jenny was peeling potatoes. He said it like you would say, "The elastic's gone out of my underwear," with a bit of surprise and wonder in his voice, as if it weren't possible, but there it was. He said, "Why don't we go to Decatur?" She almost cut her thumb on the knife, almost bloodied the potatoes. Was it possible? She gave him a stare of incredulousness, then one of suspicion. He gave them back. They looked around the yard, across the field, and then up into the hills at the trees. The trees were still green.

"It's a holiday," he said.

"It's only Wednesday," she said.

"You got to have imagination. Pretend it's Saturday."

"We don't even need anything. For instance, what would we do with these peeled potatoes?"

"Cut 'em up, fry 'em, take 'em with us, eat 'em on the way. Like crackers."

"It's midday now."

"It'll only take an hour to get there. They've got the road paved from Decatur all the way out to the Muskatatuck. We'll stop at Feathers' and get a pop."

"One of the kids might call."

"We'll call them first, get 'em to go along. We'll pick 'em up on the way."

"Well," she said, "why not?" thinking that it was 1953, that she was forty-four, that the Cold War was very cold, that it was the Fourth of July, and that perhaps the whole world might explode. It was worth taking a chance. This was a strange thing. And right in the middle of the potatoes. She felt, by agreeing, that she had suddenly thrown off all her clothes and run around the house waving her arms in the air. It left her winded, and with a blush. "Well, why not?" she said again, and Mitchell, who had been on the other side of the argument, didn't jump in to help her with that question. He just got up from his chair, like it was all settled, and patted his stomach. Still, they both felt like looking over their shoulders. Said it just like that, "Why don't we go to Decatur?" It was the most brave, audacious, unimaginable boldness. By God, they would do it. Potatoes be damned! It was their new rallying cry. "Potatoes be damned!" Jenny said, and stood up and patted her stomach. They would go. They would supplicate the household gods and go to Decatur.

112

Decatur. There was almost too much in the conception for a three-syllable word to hold it all in. It was all oxymoron, including itself out, denying its own existence, burning and freezing. It was like some dark thing, excessively bright. It was a mangled beauty, drawing you to it while you cursed yourself for wanting to look. It was a single thing unaffected by death or birth. Sunny Decatur, the sun glinting off the twin spires of the Canterbury House. Craggy Decatur, one- and two- and three-leveled—buildings, trees, and towers. Sea-circled Decatur, a dark sparkle among surges of corn and rye and tobacco. It was where all sin and grace met, where adventure rested. It was the destination of all journeys and home. It was all of these things according to the brochure the Chamber of Commerce put out. It was Atlantis and Eldorado and Hanalee and Cockaigne and Oz. It was the inferno and paradise. They would wait for weeks for the opportunity to go and then find they could have gone at any time. They would go, and there, want to return home. It was at the end of hope. And it was there below them; they could feel its nightly glow, feel the shimmer of its concrete heat on the day. It was there below them, and all they had to do to reach it was descend, their muse the Decatur Road. It was ridiculous.

They prepared for the journey. They offered grain to the goats and chickens. The dog was given burned stew, forgotten and fried on the stove. Jenny packed a dinner of corn and meat, with a jug of water and a bottle of wine four years old. "Probably vinegar by now, brine," she said. They bathed and put on fragrant clothing. They brought in all the clothes off the line and closed all the windows and doors. It was as if a storm approached. They packed a sack of groceries for one of the kids and took twenty-five dollars out of a metal box. They agreed to tell each other stories, instructive and amusing, on the way, to shorten the way. Mitchell swept out the bed of the truck and put

the food and blankets there. He broke an empty grape
Nehi bottle over the bumper of the old truck. The truck
was sway-framed, and its fenders looked like sharp bones,
knobbed knees, needle elbows. He christened it "Rosy."
And he, he was Mitchell Parks of the Thacher Knobs, and
the world needed his immediate presence. He pulled the
visor of his John Deere cap over his eyes and mounted his
vehicle. His lady got in on the other side. He looked at her.

He said, "Decatur."

She looked back and said, "Decatur."

They were ready. They would pull into the main square
on the road that led directly from their home. They would
set their lawn chairs up on the bed of the truck. They
would have to hide the wine. They would eat their
potatoes. They would watch the Fourth-of-July display,
the fireworks celebrating the night, the independence.

"Decatur," he said again.

"Or bust," she added.

They began the journey, they talked of what they
would find at the end of the way. But the road was before
them now. They knew that the journey itself, the going
over the worn and nascent paths, was all that mattered—
the simple frictional movement through time and space
that was all hope and adventure and mystery was all that
mattered, their pilgrimage. Their life, they had lately dis-
covered, was a startling series of incessant beginnings.

32

Eight-year-old Julie Olson moved downstairs into the
basement very slowly, balancing the tray of sandwiches.
She had very tight blond curls; she was very proud. It was

dark in the basement, but she could see light coming out from underneath the curtains her father had put up. She pushed them aside with her elbow and all the people sitting around the little table looked straight at her; this hurt her eyes more than the bright light did, and she had to blush.

"There's Daddy's little darlin'," her father said.

"Momma made 'em." And not knowing what to do with her hands after she gave the tray to her father, she helplessly put them over her eyes. Besides her father there were three others at the table.

Old Mrs. Hampton, the school librarian, said, "Hello, Julie," and gave her a hug.

Mr. Baker smiled at her and said, "How are you? Are you sure you didn't make these?"

Roger Simpson, younger than the others, said, "Hi," and looked at his lap.

"I've got to go now," she said, "Jimmy's waitin' on me." Her father leaned back and held the curtains open for her.

When they heard the door to the basement shut, the school librarian said, "She's a real darling, Olson. But you oughtn't to let her play with those half-breeds down the road."

Olson said, "She don't play with 'em much. Besides, they're more white than Indian anyway."

"She checked out a book on Indians the other day."

"Well, I'll watch her." And he got up and started a little fire in the old furnace. Mr. Baker took the flag out of his suitcase and spread it over the card table. Roger Simpson and Mrs. Hampton sat very still, with their hands folded in their laps, across the table from each other. Mr. Baker sat back down and Olson brought the centerpiece, a small American flag with its base screwed into a Bible, and set it on the table.

Mrs. Hampton opened the meeting. "This July twelve

meeting of the Knights of Kith is officially started. Mr. Gant could not be in attendance because of an illness. He sends his regards and this copy of *Robin Hood*. I think the first thing we need to talk about is whether we're going to let George Henderson become a Knight. The table is open to discussion."

Roger Simpson put his hand on the table and leaned forward. "I'll speak for him. He's hated niggers almost as long as me." And he leaned back and laughed.

Mr. Baker said Henderson had always wanted to come to the meetings. He, Mr. Baker, had told him their beliefs, and Henderson had agreed to all of them wholeheartedly.

Mrs. Hampton said, "Olson?"

"Fine with me."

"Okay, then, Mr. Baker, bring him along next time. Tell him it costs thirty dollars to join."

Roger Simpson lit up again, "I've got a little number to share with y'all." He sat a chrome twenty-two caliber revolver on the table.

Olson said, "That thing ain't loaded, is it?"

"You damn fool!" screamed the old librarian. "All our cars parked out front and you bring in a gun."

Simpson put both of his hands in his pockets. "Well, hell, when we gonna do something? Tell me that. All we ever do is meet and talk. It would be easy. I've been practicing. Only one of you would have to come along, to drive. It would just take a minute. Easy."

"You damn fool. I don't ever want to see that thing again. We'll do our business when I say. At no other time. We'll be heroes." Her pale skin, like a sheet of onion-skin paper, seemed to grow raw as she spoke.

"All right, all right, let's just calm down." Olson lit a cigarette. Baker shifted in his chair. Olson began again. "Let's just calm down. We'll start the ceremony and get out of here. Roger, put the gun back in your pocket."

"It would be easy," he said.

Mr. Baker reached into his suitcase and drew out a handful of pamphlets. "I went over to the college in Decatur, to the administration building. I'm going to start going there regular. There were all these papers about a nigger college fund and how to give money to it." He got up from the table, taking the pamphlets, and threw them into the furnace. Everyone clapped and he smiled when he sat back down at the table. They all turned to Olson.

"Well, this is the best thing I ever did. I went to the Popehead church like I wanted to join. The guy there gave me one of their special songbooks and a whole stack of fliers. I told him I already had my own Bible. Get it? So then I told him I wanted to get songbooks for my mother and father and wife and kids." Olson got up and went beyond the curtains. He brought back a stack of hymnals and literature, showed them to everyone, then threw them one at a time through the little open door of the furnace. The others clapped at each toss.

The old librarian took another book out of her purse and placed it beside the copy of *Robin Hood*. "Mr. Gant wanted me to say the reason he sends this book is because Robin Hood, essentially, was a communist, taking from those who worked hard for their money and giving it to those who didn't. I had never thought of it that way before, but he explained it. I've brought another copy of *Little Red*. I tell the school board the children keep stealing the books so I can order more to burn."

"You steal from your own library?" Olson laughed.

"It has to be done. Children are very impressionable. No use in starting a big fuss over it." They all laughed. Mrs. Hampton threw the books into the furnace and another round of applause followed.

Roger Simpson took three books out from underneath his chair and set them on the table. "I went to the library in Lexington when I was there last week. They wouldn't let me check these out, they're real old, so I had to sneak them out. Easy as you please. Right past the old snipe at the door. These are foreign-language Bibles, translated out of American. This one here is German, this one French, and this book is the Twenty-third Psalm in one hundred and one different languages." He looked at them all and smiled.

The rest of them just sat there. Then Mrs. Hampton rose up from the table, pointing her long arm and finger at him. "You damn fool. The Bible was written in Greek. Don't you know anything? You damn fool."

She had caught him by surprise again and his breath caught midway to his lungs. He stood up and waved his arms, staggering back, away from the table. His right hand found the lump in his pocket and he pulled the revolver out, became suddenly very calm. He lifted his arm, his hand loose, then firm. For a moment the two hands, his and hers, almost touched, were almost a mirror image, except for the gun, of that old Michelangelo painting. He fired through her open mouth, once. She sat back down, hardly as if she had been shot, as if she were a sheet of paper the bullet didn't even bother to flutter as it passed through.

"See that?" Roger Simpson said, putting the pistol down gently on the tabletop. "Easy as you please."

33

There was always, of course, this day-to-day argument with the earth, to make it say tobacco instead of darnel or milkweed or even beans. It was early morning, intimations of dawn in the east, and he was moving quickly along the rows of knee-high plants. His pants legs and boots were dew-saturated and heavy; whenever he brushed a plant with the hoe handle a fine spray of water coated him anew. It was midsummer, and weeds grew six inches a day; let them go for a week and they would top the tobacco. It was best to get them in the morning, when the ground was soft and least expected the hoe. He stopped at the end of a row, knocked the dirt off the ground blade, and paused to watch the sun rise up over the Appalachians. Although he was still lean and brown-skinned, his brow was already sweating. Each morning he reached that point when it was time to stop rushing, stop trying to beat the heat and slow down to a steady swing and sweat, a second or two earlier than the day before. He watched the sun rise, and heard the pulse of the earth and the ocean in its rising. In another few moments the glare would be unbearable, and not until the last few seconds of sunset would he be able to look at the sun again. During the day he had to look at the earth. And he had settled into it, the breathing of the day, had fought off the morning disgust of losing the farm, and had settled into his work when it all started.

The back door slammed and he looked up to see Jenny, at first walking, but then hopping and finally running toward him. She came close at top speed, breathless, tripped over a clod and hit Mitchell in the chest with the full force of her flailing body. She lay sprawled on top of him, panting. "Shoot a gun off behind my back and see if I jump, see if I'm startled. I will never be startled again after today," she says.

He says, "What? . . . What?" he says.

"We got company," she whispers, clamping her hand over Mitchell's gasping mouth.

"Get off of me," he squeezes between her sweating fingers. They stand up and brush off their clothes; Mitchell tries to set straight a broken plant. "What company?" he asks, since Jenny won't go on.

She says, "Three of the strangest humans on this earth. I think three. Two in the house, one still in the car outside.

Want to talk to you and me together. That Holland is one of them. The other is a woman and the one in the car is Reverend Washer, but I am not sure because he's hiding in the back seat.

He says, "What? . . . What?"

"Come with me right now." And she drags him through the tobacco to the back door, but before going in whispers a sirocco in his baffled ear: "Now be calm and act natural."

"What? . . . What?" he says.

"You are going to have a hell of a lot of explaining to do when this is over," she thrusts into his absolute bewilderment as the door slams behind them. Jenny swathes her skirt with both palms and Mitchell rubs his nose as they walk into the front room.

There on the parlor sofa is Holland with his dull eyes and he is holding hands with Marguerite Green, who is wearing a silk kimono with birds and cattails on it. The kimono shows a healthy expanse of her pearly bosom. Holland is wearing a new black suit accented with an American-flag lapel pin. Out on the porch a dog is peering in through the window at Holland. Farther out, in the driveway, the Minister Washer is peering out of a car window, absentmindedly smoothing his red-striped tie.

"Mitchell," Jenny says, "sit down here and stop your staring." Mitchell slumps down next to her on the love seat. "Mitchell," she goes on, "you've read some of Miss Green's book reviews in the paper."

"Yes, ma'am?" he says.

"She writes under a pen name, of course—Cleveland Charlton."

"Oh, yes," he adds, thinking, why, they're holding hands.

"Miss Green, in her own words, has been the county courtesan for some years past."

"Oh?"

"A lady of the evening, Mitchell."

120

"Oh. What?"

"She has made a living by providing services for payment."

"I don't know her at all, Jenny. Maybe she's mistaken me for one of the boys—Henry or Steve—but I don't know you at all, do I, Miss Green?"

"No, you don't, Mr. Parks." And she smiles sweetly.

"Jesus, holy Christ, no, I don't know her, Jenny."

"That's not what we're talking about, Mitchell. Miss Green has told me this because she and Mr. Holland have asked a favor of us and feel that we should know. She has decided to give up her career."

"Well, like I said, that don't mean nothing to me, Jenny. Hello, Jim."

He nodded.

Miss Green folded her hands in her retired lap.

Jenny asked if anyone would like coffee.

No, they wouldn't, but thank you very much anyway.

Jesus, holy Christ, no, I don't know her, Jenny, he thinks.

"They would like us to act as witnesses," Jenny said, "to their marriage."

"We've brought the minister along, Mr. Parks," Holland said.

"We would like to have the wedding outside," Miss Green added, "but understand if you choose the backyard."

Mitchell looked around the room, at his hand, at the dog on the porch, and the minister peering over the back seat of the car, and then at Jenny. "No," he said, "the front yard will be better; I've had practice there."

Holland asked, "I'd be pleased if you would act as my best man and also give away the bride, Mr. Parks. And if Mrs. Parks would be the maid of honor. Of course, you would have to sign the wedding certificate also. If we ask too much, we understand."

121

"No," Jenny said, "it's all fine; we'd be honored, wouldn't we, Mitchell?" Thinking, my boys?

Holland rose up from the sofa, moved slowly to the front door and motioned to the minister. The Minister Washer sneaked brightly into the front room, all teeth and tie.

"Glad to see you, Mrs. Parks, Mr. Parks. Is everything set then? Beautiful day for a ceremony, isn't it? Yes, Lord, what a day. Why . . ."

"Oh, Duncan, please calm down," says Miss Green.

"Yes, yes, fine, Marguerite, Miss Green. Well, shall we get it over with?"

Everyone nodded and went out onto the grass of the front lawn. The minister set himself up on the front porch and the dog circled twice near his shoe and finally sat on it. He began the ceremony, but Holland reached out and stopped him. "Marguerite has written our vows, Mr. Washer."

"What's that?"

"I've written our own vows, Duncan. Would you please use them? Here."

"Well, I suppose. But I can't read this. It's in some kind of foreign tongue."

"It's French, Mr. Washer," Holland says, "we are going to do it in a romance language. You use that. Get through it the best you can. We'll repeat them."

"Well, does it say anything about God in here?"

"Yes, Duncan," Miss Green assured.

"Well, I suppose."

Jenny and Mitchell stood by as the minister hobbled through the French and the bride and groom turned it on as from a tap. When the vows were over, Holland, fifteen years older than his forty-year-old wife, leaned over and kissed her. The minister got back in the car, and the dog hopped in after him.

Mitchell asked, "Y'all gonna live at your place, Jim?"

Holland said, "No."

And Mrs. Holland added, "We are moving to New Orleans. We're going to open a pet hotel."

Then they said thank you and got back in the car too.

The minister leaned out of the car window and yelled, "Nothing need be said of this if you've a mind."

Mitchell nodded. The car turned around, drove out of the yard, and disappeared around the bend. It had all happened in less than an hour.

They stood together in the front yard.

"You don't suppose," Jenny said, "that we will ever tell anyone about this?"

"No," he said, "we will keep it just for ourselves. We won't share it with anyone."

"And my boys?"

"Who knows?"

She says, "I doubt it. She would not be their type."

"I used to think we missed some things living up here like we do."

"I will never be startled again."

"Well, I've got tobacco to tend to."

"Yes," she adds, "there is wash to be brought in."

34

Snakes didn't bother him at all, and he could let a spider crawl up and down his arm all day. What it was was dogs. Little dogs, big dogs, French names or not, he didn't like them. It probably had something to do with an incident in his childhood, but he could not recall anything in particular. His mother said they got him a puppy on his third birthday, and instead of hugging the puppy he screamed and wet his pants. It was just a phobia; everyone had one or two phobias. But dogs were basically good, kind-hearted animals: man's best friend. He told himself this over and over, standing in the Decatur Road, twenty feet from a German shepherd who had trotted out to the center of the road, sat down in his path, and bared its teeth. It was very hot out on the road. This standoff couldn't last much longer. He folded his arms. It was a very big German shepherd. The army uses them for attack dogs.

It is not often that you see someone walking down this road these days. If this guy were in a car, he would probably go out of his way to run me down. Or at least honk at me. And all I would be able to do would be bark. But this is like the old days when people walked down this road every day. I was respected then, people knew me. Used to call my name and throw me something, a piece of sandwich or a bone, and I'd let them go on. But now, often as not, some jerk is throwing a can or bottle at me. This guy ought to have something to eat in that backpack. I'll take that and maybe even a bite of his leg before he gets by. I am old, and the times are changing, but I'll take my due, corner one more memory.

This dog isn't moving. He doesn't even bark, just bares his teeth and sits there in the road. If I was in a car, I'd probably wreck trying to miss him. I got to get on down the highway. It'll be dark before long. Well, I can make a move, face him down. I could use a good stick. Maybe best just to wait him out. He can't sit there all day. Wait a minute. Here comes a truck.

The man stuck his arm and thumb out, but the truck didn't stop. It was getting dark. The dog moved over to the side of the road where he was standing. Well, all right, he would wait him out. This dog would have to go home and eat sometime soon. This sounded reasonable. He shifted his pack and sat down against a fence post.

Walk across America, his dad had said. He watched the dog.

Just watch him. If he starts to get on the truck, I'll rush him, maybe get a foot. But no, the truck's going on. Okay, if this is going to be a waiting game, I can handle that. It's getting dark. I'll probably have to forget about supper. The thing is just to stay awake and keep an eye on him. He might try jumping that fence and sneaking around.

I'll probably have to wait just a little while longer and he'll get up and go home.

The thing is just to watch him, stay awake and watch him. But it's probably all right to rest my head a little. It's very warm.

My God, he's settling in for the night. You can only barely make him out in the dark. Maybe he's asleep. Maybe he's not. Maybe I could just sneak past him. It's pretty dark.

It's very warm tonight. He's still there, isn't he, against the post? Yes. Just a little rest then, maybe.

I know that dog is asleep. I could just get up real easy and soft and sneak by him. I could really do that. Oh, Christ, what's the use. It's just a mile back to that crossroad. It's another fourteen miles to Decatur, anyway. I'll start out on some other road. I'll bet there are road dogs all over America.

It's morning. Where am I? I'm out by the road. The GUY!? He's gone!
The dog got up slowly and strained his eyes, looking down the Decatur Road, first one way, then the other. Far away, just a tiny brown speck on the shimmering road, a car was coming.

35

"Climacteric," the old nurse at the doctor's office had said, calmly, placing her hand on her bosom, "you have atoned for that old apple sin." And then she laughed.

She felt this last slow flow of blood most acutely at night, when the moon paused at each pane of her bedroom window. She lay on her back, one hand reaching up to the top of the headboard and turning one of the five pegs which stood for her children. She turned them around and around; the pegs were worn and loose in their holes from her turning. Mitchell rolled over, turning his back to her. With a quick teardrop down her cheek and a flush of heat she swung her elbow at him and he grunted in his sleep. Then this was over, and there was again only the aloneness, the soft sense of the blood's ebbing.

Her extended hand grew weak and heavy from the blood's upward climb. She dropped her arm back down to her side. The moon, she knew, had lost its memory in its pausing. She felt her life's blood flowing away. And then, as suddenly as it had begun, the ebbing ceased. Everything was very still inside of her. This had only happened to her five times before. She could only relate this to those other times. It was as if she were waiting for a birth. She felt within herself the tug of the earth, the old birth urge, but the pulse and drumming of the species was not there. The species no longer needed her.

She brought her feet up so that her knees raised and spread the sheet. And she lay there, very still. She dreamed a dream: She and Mitchell were walking along the furrows of a long field that he had been working and sweating in all day. They came, in their walking, to a hedge of bushes and ferns that stretched as far as they could see in both directions. But before them, the ferns opened and revealed a white picket gate, and in front of the gate rabbits were hopping about, feeding on clover. The rabbits looked up and saw them, then ran to the little gate, stacked themselves on top of each other precariously and opened it. There was a garden, with fruit trees and vines growing full and randomly. She went through the gate, past the playing rabbits, back into the garden. There were strawberries on the ground and golden peaches, like sunsets, at her shoulders. Mist came up from a meandering brook, and it seemed that everything was wet, glistening with mist and dew. She turned to Mitchell and found he was not with her, but still standing beyond the gate in the dust of the furrow. She called him but he said, "I can't." Then she noticed that the rabbits outside the gate had turned into wolves. She saw Mitchell turning away. The bushes were starting to grow back across the open space. She only glanced at the strawberries as she ran through the gate, screaming as she ran through the pack of wolves and the thick wet hedge.

She woke up sweating, bathed in her own fluid, holding her knees tight against her chest, baffled and wide-eyed at the dawn. But the dream, the garden, the wolves were gone, forgotten like the pain of birth.

36

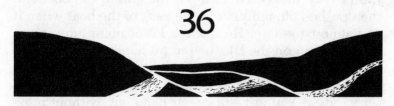

He pushed the curtains back and saw that it was already morning outside. He quickly picked up his shirt and pants, put them on, and hurried downstairs; but halfway to the kitchen he slowed down because he remembered that his dad had promised. It was his first time to be going. His father said he could carry the bird bag. The coffee smell was already in the stairwell, and when he reached the kitchen he saw that his mom was making breakfast. She said, "Morning, Pewee," and then his dad came out of their bedroom with his hunting clothes on. His mom was still in her robe.

"Do you want me to go get in the car, Dad? I'm ready."

"Eat you some breakfast first, and where are your shoes? Can't go hunting without shoes."

They had put the canoe on top of the car the night before. He got in the car and rolled down his window. His Mom came out on the porch in her robe with her arms folded. She said, "Pewee, you remember about always walking behind your father."

He said, "Okay," real fast and then she went back inside rubbing her arms.

They drove out of town a long way, to a place where the road went close to a big lake. His dad let him carry the gun down to the shore while he carried the canoe. It was a big day, the sky was open and blue, and the air was empty of wind. The lake was smooth. He got into the canoe first, stepping very carefully to the front seat. The boat waddled from side to side as he walked. It wasn't very steady. His dad put the gun in the boat and then pushed off, jumping in the back of the boat when it was almost too late. He made a lot of noise jumping in like that. Out on the lake he put his hand in the water as his dad paddled and watched the little wake it made. It was something. It was like sticking your hand out of the car window. You just stuck your hand out, without moving it, and the water pushed against it. The water was clear where it hit his hand, but blue everywhere else.

This was fun, putting your hand in the water that looked very still.

At the far side of the lake they pulled the canoe onto shore and started walking. He remembered to walk behind his dad. They came to the edge of an old cornfield and his father said to be quiet. This was something that went with hunting, being quiet. He spent the quiet time playing with a stick and looking into the empty bird bag. Then his dad said, "Okay." So he looked up. And out over the cornfield, very near them, a bird was gliding down out of the sky. Then his dad jumped up and raised the gun and fired all at once. The gun was very loud in the quiet. The bird balled itself up and dropped.

His dad walked out to the bird very quickly, taking big steps over the corn stubble. The bird was brown and gray, but some of its feathers were turned up in a funny way, and they were white underneath. "He's a fat one; me and him both knew this cornfield," his father said. Then he put the bird in Pewee's bag. The bird wasn't too heavy, he thought, to be fat.

"Hope Momma has lunch made when we get back," his dad said, and Pewee said, "yeah." His dad pushed them off again. The lake was still very smooth. He took the bird bag off his shoulder and laid it down very gently behind him in the boat. He wanted to let his hand trail in the water some more. He put it in the water and watched it for a moment, then he put his chin on the very front of the boat and closed his eyes. He liked the feel of the air on his face and the water on his hand. His father said, "Yes, sir, that's some bird for your first trip; Momma will be real proud of that." He kept his eyes closed and saw again the bird floating down out of the sky. Then he nearly turned the boat over, screaming and jerking his hand out of the water. Something had tried to get his hand. He looked at his hand and then looked back in the water. There was a yellow leaf floating on the surface. It was the leaf that had hit his hand, he knew, but still he could not stop shaking, or stop rubbing his hand on his shirt. He had thought that something had tried to get him. But after a while it was all right. It was just a leaf. He put his hand back in the water, but he kept his eyes open, watching over the smooth expanse of the water in front of him. He had to watch that. He couldn't let anything surprise him again.

37

It was August, and the three of them sat on the front porch in the afternoons, avoiding August. Under the porch, with the oscillating fan, it was still June. Mitchell and Jenny worked in the mornings and late evenings, when it was early June and at times May and October. But the old lady liked to sit on the porch all day, right in front of the oscillating electric fan, so that it swept past her every few seconds. The fan had three speeds. In the morning it would be on low and by noon she had it turned up to high. It was on medium for only a little while.

She said, "Have you got the dishes done yet, Jenny?" And she raised a fist, like a piece of veined quartz, to her cheek.

"Yes, Momma, they're all done."

Mitchell said, "That fan all right? You want me to move it for you?"

"No, thank you, Mitchell. It's all right."

"Well, okay," he said. "If you want me to move it, just tell me."

"All right, I will."

For six years, after Jenny's father died and her mother came to live with them, there were these afternoons on the porch. There was the hum and hush of the fan and the heat of the afternoon that put Mitchell to sleep on the porch swing. There was the arc and sweep of the fan, flapping the corners of the newspaper Mitchell read and dropped under the swing. And there was her mother, rocking quietly back and forth. Even in the heat of the day she spread a small blanket across her knees. The oscillating fan, in its slow, calm turning, moved across them all. It gave motion to the swing Mitchell lay on, made the chains creak. It moved across the old lady and brought her back to life, blowing her white hair back and lifting the collar of her dress. And then it shifted to Jenny, and it made her think the fan has just been on Mitchell and Momma and now it is on me so good and now it will go back to them. This is how it was in the afternoons.

Toward evening Mitchell would wake up and groan and push himself up out of the swing. He would say, "What time is it?" and then ask the old lady if she wanted anything. Then he would sit back down after stretching and say, "Well, I've got to hoe the garden," or "Well, I've got to feed the stock." But he wouldn't get up for another half hour, not till Jenny went in the house to fix dinner. During the half hour they would watch Jenny's mother. She was dying, and it showed most in the late afternoons.

Her father had died very early, at fifty-nine, in a car crash. It was a spectacular accident, and he was killed instantly. It had happened a day before his sixtieth birthday, and Jenny took it as a refusal to enter into old age, although there were no signs that the wreck wasn't an accident.

Her mother lived alone for five years. In the late summer of 1953 she had a stroke, and needing attention, she moved out to the farm. There, she took life for its time of day, but continued to have occasional small strokes. The doctor said the two arteries to her brain were closed to a pin's diameter. He couldn't operate on one artery because the other didn't carry enough blood to keep her alive. As it was, most of her memory was gone. She remembered only fragments of events, repeated habitual statements, forgot even the time of day. She required almost as much care as a child.

Each succeeding stroke brought about other changes. The old lady, losing daily her reason and intellect, became, instead of increasingly bitter and hard to deal with, more amiable. She became, in fact, Jenny thought, a better, happier person than she used to be.

It was hard for Jenny to think, watching her mother rock before the fan, that the old lady was not thinking. But she knew that if she had a thought, it would actually startle her out of the rhythm of the rocker and the fan and her heart. At the moment there was nothing there.

Jenny folded her book over the porch railing, and looking past her mother, asked Mitchell what he wanted for dinner.

"A big glass of iced tea," he said, "I just want a big cool drink of iced tea. In one of those big glasses." Then he got up and said, "I'll be out in the barn," and passing the old lady, he patted her on the knee.

The old woman looked up and watched Mitchell cross the yard and go into the barn. She stopped her rocking and with an effort turned her head to Jenny, saying, "I don't think so." Then she smoothed the blanket back over her knees and continued to rock.

How odd, Jenny thought, how odd, how odd.

It was a long time ago. It was in August, late in the day, and it had been raining and it had stopped. She had walked out into the yard and said yes, she would, yes. And Mitchell had come running, slipping, had made a general fool of himself, so that she had held the screen door tight

132

with both hands and he could not get to her. She had told him to go home and he finally had. She watched him walk back down the Decatur Road as far as she could see that night. Then she closed the big door softly and locked it. The house was dark and quiet, she had to feel her way through the kitchen and living room to her parents' bedroom. Her mother was sitting up in bed, reading. Her father was beside her, smoking.

He said, "That boy hurt himself on the gate? What was all that racket?"

She walked over and knelt at the foot of their bed, her elbows on the mattress and her chin on her fist. "I am going to marry Mitchell Parks," she said. "He asked me and I am going to."

Her father sat up, put out his cigarette and said, "Well, what about that."

Then her mother put her book down and said, "I don't think so." She said it very simply.

Jenny stood up. She didn't know what to do. She refused to ask why. There were no reasons. Then her mother picked the book back up and began to read. Jenny's lips started to tremble. But before she could even turn to her father, he did a strange thing. He got up out of the bed, went into the bathroom, then came back out and said, "You've thought this out, sugar? This isn't a rash thing?"

"No, Daddy, I mean yes. I mean I want to."

"Then you go ahead."

It was the first time he hadn't backed her mother up. And he had gotten out of the bed to do it. Her mother reached up and turned out the light. She turned on her side and said, "Jenny, go on to bed." So she left. She went into her own bedroom and got into bed, flushed with the victory over her mother. She thought about Mitchell and the night and the next morning. But there was something else too. Her mother reaching up and turning out the light and turning over. And her father, as she left, standing in the middle of the room in his shorts. Lord, she had thought, he didn't have to go as far as getting out of the bed.

She looked over at the old woman in the rocker enjoying the fan. It was a curious thing, to feel sad about an old victory that had to happen. There had been more and more of them, victories over her mother, after that night. Some of them seemed very shallow in the afternoon light. It was a fact. There were some people in the world you just didn't get along with. Sometimes one of them happened to be your mother, that's all.

Jenny got up to fix dinner. The old lady stopped her rocking and looked at her again. "Have you got the dishes done yet, Jenny?"

"Yes, Momma, they're done."

Some people died very quickly, others wandered into old age. Sometimes you forgot you were born: that was what made you think you wouldn't die. But her mother was here now, and she remembered. The stroke, actually, might have been a good thing. Her mother became, really, an altogether different person from what she was.

"Well, honey, are the dishes all done?"

The fan swept past, pushing the heat of August over them, blowing the old lady's white hair back from her quartz face.

"Yes, Momma, they're all done now."

38

You are sure, first thing, that the Painted, the Gobi, the Sahara have nothing over the Decatur Road in August. What the road lacks in sand and cactus and scorpions, it makes up for with blacktop and broken glass and Mack trucks. Second thing you are sure of is that death could not be far away. And as if put there to goad you, there is a big billboard that reads, THE MIAMI MOTEL TV POOL ONLY 12 MILES, with a girl in a sleek red bathing suit just about to dive into the word POOL. The thing to do is to start sticking that thumb out. Get it out and keep it out. You might not get anything; you might get a hog van; you might get a Cadillac. It doesn't matter. The hope and possibility of that thumb is all that's important. The kindness of the world is in that thumb. Keep it out.

In the meantime there are just you and the road. The air is thick like the hair on a collie, and breathing is like drinking a cup of mattress stuffing. The road is straight and long before you, patched with mirages and shimmering in the distance with sweat. The stores and houses along the roadside hover in the humidity, threatening to give in to the idleness of the day and simply disappear. Every once in a while a hard-shelled grasshopper will blitz and smack into your arm or cheek. But there is nothing to do but keep on walking. You can stop at a store or gas station and get a pop, but that only helps for a hundred yards or so. Then your mouth gets full of hair again, your eyes sting. The sweating has never stopped. The rocks and things you've picked up along the way only seem heavy and sharp in your pocket. You take them out and they've lost the color and shape they had in the morning. You try an impossible shot with your beautiful rock, aiming at the long thin razor strand of new barbed wire glinting in the sun. You take the pop bottle out of your back pocket and give it a heave down into a dry creek bottom. It's not worth the dime to carry it. And all this time you've got your thumb sticking out into the thick air like it smelled bad.

So maybe, after you've decided there isn't a friend left on the American highway and that death is truly yours to have and hold, a truck throttles and gears down in front of you, crunching the gravel on the side of the road. You find you still have the energy to lope up to the cab and climb in. The guy, a funny-looking guy eating peanuts (who has a small electric fan mounted on the dash pointed right at his face: an absolute genius), asks where you're going. You tell him Decatur and he says he can take you five miles down the road. You decide that God exists. The truck gears back up and there is wind all over the place. Pop bottles roll around the floorboard of the truck and smack into the door when the truck makes a curve. There is about a half inch of dirt there on the floor too. You turn the vent window in so you get that hot August blast. The road moves by very quickly now, and you can see the cattle out in the fields and the brilliant white houses and black barns. You can see down below you the road ditch, the broken glass, the grasshoppers, the dry fescue and the barbed wire singing by. You can see the shimmering air. And you figure you would have made it even if the truck hadn't come along. You sit back and munch on a peanut and are sure of that.

39

"Hey, Tom, let's go fishing."
  "I want to finish here, Grandpa."
  "What you doing?"
  "Building a device which communicates by electromagnetic waves transmitted through space."
  "It says here 'A-One Radio Kit.'"

"Don't move anything, Grandpa. I have it spread out on the table the way I want it."

"Sure you don't want to go fishing? There's only two weeks left before you have to go home."

"I want to finish this, Grandpa."

"Well, I'll just help you then. What's this?"

"Don't bend the prongs on it, Grandpa. It won't fit in the board. It's a transistor."

"What's that?"

"It's an active semiconductor device having three or more electrodes."

"They left all the tubes out of your kit here; we're going to have to take it back."

"Grandpa, that's what transistors are; they perform almost all the functions of tubes, including rectification and amplification."

"And they're that little. Where'd you learn to talk like that?"

"I make a habit of memorizing definitions."

"You got a dog out at your place in California?"

"No."

"Ought to get you a dog. Maybe we can get you one to take back with you. I grew up with a dog named Zeke. He was an awful good dog. Haven't had a better one. Big black Labrador with some German shepherd in him. Had too good a soul to be born human. I've missed that dog since the day he was gone. Always will, I guess. Awful good dog."

"Grandpa, watch out, that soldering iron is hot."

"All right. Did I ever tell you about Steve Trater and his dogs?"

"Huh? No."

"Well, he used to get mad at them so, and his wife wouldn't let him beat them. So whenever they really got him mad he would tie them to a short rope under a

137

dropping bois d'arc tree, you know, a horseapple tree. It would drive those dogs insane. They could never get a moment's peace of mind. Wherever a dog would lie down, he'd stand a good chance of getting struck by a dropping horseapple. You know how heavy them things are. Sometimes in the middle of the night you'd hear the most woeful yeep and yowl coming out of Trater's hollow and you'd know a dog was going crazy. He ruined a lot of dogs that way. But the ones that came through it were like steel. What's this here?"

"Huh? Oh, that's a diode."

"What's that?"

"It's a two-terminal electronic device that will conduct electricity much more easily in one direction than in the other."

"Hey, it don't snow much out there in Los Angeles, does it?"

"Nope."

"You know we had a snow here in 1942 that beat every snow I'd ever seen. It snowed three feet in one afternoon and a night. That next morning me and your daddy—I guess he was about your age—no, he was older, about fifteen—well, that next morning we went out to check the pigs. Come to find out the shed they stayed in got completely blown down. We dug down through the snow to it, expecting to find seven or eight frozen pigs, but there wasn't a pig to be found. We didn't know what to make of it. We looked all around the barn and the house. No pigs. Then we looked through the woods around the farm. No pigs. We were walking back across the field when we noticed a thin column of steam rising up out of the snow. There was a hole in the snow and the steam rose up out of it. We walked over to the hole and there was no mistaking it. That steam was pig breath. We got shovels and started to dig. Down at about three and a half feet were seven of the coziest pigs you ever saw. We had to carry them one at a time into the house to thaw, but every one of them was alive. One little baby pig did get his snout frostbit, but that was nothing, considering his whole life. Beat any pig happening I ever heard of. You ever hear of anything like that?"

"Huh? Oh, no, Grandpa, that's real interesting."

"You want to go down to Perry's? I'll get you a pop."

"No, I think I'll just try to finish the radio, Grandpa."

"What's this little thing here?"

"That's a capacitor."

"Oh."

"It's a device that consists essentially of two conducting surfaces separated by an insulating material or dialectric such as air, paper, mica, or glass. It stores electrical energy, blocks the flow of direct current, and permits the flow of alternating current."

"How about that. All right in there. Science is amazing, isn't it."

"Yeah. The President says we're going to the moon. I want to be the first astronaut to go to the moon."

"The moon?"

"Oh yeah. It's quite feasible with rocket power. It would just be a matter of days."

"Some adventure."

"Not really."

"One time when I was about your age, me and two of my best friends decided to go swimming. It was the hottest part of the summer, like it is now, and it hadn't rained in a good while. Even the Muskatatuck was down to a trickle. One of the boys knew of a pond up in the hills that still had plenty of water. So we hiked all the way up to it, through the driest country you ever saw. We saw the pond down at the bottom of a little slope. George Hamilton was one of the boys. He was always quicker than any of us. He took off down that slope, flinging his clothes off and screaming to boot. He dived in head-first and came up out in the middle still yelling. It was all he could do to tell us not to come in, that something was stinging him. We had to pull him out with a long pole. He had been snake-bit twenty-seven times. He was a good guy, George Hamilton. Faster than all of us. He said, 'Mitch, don't jump in.' "

"Grandpa, would you hand me that packet of resistors? It's right there. Yeah."

"What do these do?"

"Resistors are components made of a material that has a specified resistance, or opposition to the flow of electrical current."

"You need me to do anything?"

"No, thanks."

"Your mom tells me there's lots of traffic out there in Los Angeles. Lot of cars."

"Yeah."

"Got some big highways, I guess."

"Some of them have six lanes."

"Don't say. Most I've ever seen is four lanes. Got four lanes in Lexington. You got many opossums in California?"

"None that I know of."

"That's good. Opossums and roads don't go together. Once when I was on a trip to Lexington, I saw a possum loaded down with its young trying to cross that four-lane road. She got hit in the hindquarters crossing the first lane. But she got up, dragging her back half with her front half. She gathered up what young she could and started out again. She crossed the second and third lane, dragging herself, and just when I thought she might make it, a truck caught her in the gravel. Roads and opossums. That night I went home and prayed for everyone I could ever remember."

"Yeah."

"You know, Tom, your father is my son."

"Yeah, I know."

"My son is your father."

"Uh-huh."

"Time and distance don't mean much to you, do they? KID?"

"I'm only thirteen, you old coot."

"Oh, SURE!"

"GRANDMA!!"

40

You can see a cop coming from miles off; there is almost a mile of level, straight-as-an-arrow blacktop, two smooth lanes and flat fields on either side. God couldn't have built a better drag strip than the Decatur Road at the eleven-mile marker.

Harrison Stork works at the supermarket in Decatur. He is seventeen, a member of the Thespian Club, a wearer of black high-top tennis shoes. He still mourns for Buddy Holly and the Big Bopper. He is standing at the register and in walks Betty Maynard, bombshell. Harrison shifts his tie and makes sure the tongues of his sneakers stick out over the cuffs of his jeans. He is ready. He hasn't looked at Betty since she walked in the store but knows by heart the pattern she usually takes through the aisles. Past the vegetables and fruit, where she always steals a few grapes, around the soft drinks and potato chips, past the meat counter, and finally over to the bread aisle, where she picks up a loaf of white bread. Harrison counts to three and looks up with a smile. It is Tony Palatucci, T-shirt and a burr, standing behind Betty, one hand draped over her soft shoulder.

"Hey, Stork, how's it going there. How 'bout a free pack of Camels?"

Harrison hates the word "Stork." "You know I can't, Tony. Hi, Betty."

"Hey, Harrison. Did you see us drive up? Tony's got his car all fixed up."

"Yeah, Stork, a '32 roadster with a Packard up front. Really moves. Fastest around."

Harrison rings up the white bread. "Twelve cents, Betty. Maybe not so fast, Tony. I've got a Caddy, you know." Betty looks up.

"A Caddy?"

"Well, it's my parents', but . . ."

Then Tony: "Can you get it tonight? We'll have us a run out on the strip."

"Oh no, no I . . ."

"Why not?"

"Well, I . . ."

And then Betty: "C'mon, Harrison."

"Well, it'll have to be after work, about eleven."

"See you at the strip, Stork." So Tony puts his arm around Betty, kisses her ear, the soft part on the bottom, Harrison notices, and they walk out, Tony saying, "What about that Stork, huh?"

"Yeah," Betty says.

Harrison Stork got his job when his dad, the town's banker, said Harrison would never make it as a banker and asked Mr. Garrison, the market manager, to hire his son. "We're just not anything alike," said the fat banker to his slim son, patting him on the shoulder sadly. Harrison felt the burden of guilt was his. And now, here he was once again, letting his parents down, rolling the black Cadillac silently down the driveway to the street. He tried to push the car farther down the block, but it was too heavy. He felt the street lamps were unusually bright tonight, like spotlights almost. He started the engine of the big car and looked at his parents' bedroom window to see if the light came on. It didn't. He was in the clear.

He drove slowly out of town and out the Decatur Road, testing the accelerator at odd moments, planning strategy, and worrying. The most important thing was not to wreck the car. Then, not to get caught by the cops. Jesus, he was already calling the police "cops." This was all wrong. But he would only do it this once. All the guys did it.

Tony and Betty were off to the side of the road waiting. They lined the two cars up and Tony gave instructions.

"Okay, Stork," Betty rides with me and says go. It's a mile race, to the mile-marker up there. No crowding, stay in your lane with that tank. Ready?"

Harrison crouched low in his seat, "Ready."

Tony brake-jacked his car up on its front end, engine roaring, the back end bobbing. Harrison put the Caddy in neutral and revved up the engine. Betty leaned out of Tony's car and yelled, "On your mark, get set, GO!"

The roadster shot forward; Harrison slipped the Cadillac's column shift down into DRIVE and stepped on the gas. To his utter amazement the big car seemed to lift a foot off the ground. He was alongside the roadster before he knew it, fighting the g-forces that pushed him back into the plush seat. Then he saw the headlights of Tony's car in his rear-view mirror as he passed the mile-marker. It had been easy. He had won. "What a car!" he screamed. And he banged the Cadillac's dash with his fist, slapped the seat next to him and nearly drove off the road. He stopped the car and waited for Tony and Betty to pull alongside. He would be gracious in his victory. But they didn't pull up; he saw the roadster turn behind him and head back to Decatur. He sat there for a moment and then turned the car around and drove home at a careful forty-five miles an hour. He hated Tony Palatucci.

Three years later, home from college where he was a drama major, Harrison sat at the kitchen table looking through a box of old family pictures with his mom. His father was still at the bank. Most of the pictures were of his parents' friends when they were his age. But he came upon one, his mother handed it to him saying, "Look at this," that sent shudders all the way through him. It was a snapshot of his mother and father in front of a car. His father had on a T-shirt, and there was a pack of cigarettes rolled up in one sleeve. His arm was draped over his mother's shoulder. She, he couldn't help but think it, looked remarkably like old Betty Maynard from high school. The car they stood in front of was a 1936 Plymouth coupe, his dad's. He had heard his dad talking about the car before, but he had never mentioned one thing. There was a huge black eight ball painted on the door. "Your father was a terror on the roads in his day." His mother smiled.

It all came back, his three-year-old victory on the Decatur Road. Seeing his father like that made him feel queer all over. It was very strange. It explained a lot. It brought glee to his heart, healed that old wound. He would go back to college and change his major to banking. He realized, for the first time, how exactly like his father he really was. A regular chip off the old block. Stork smiled, lifted his foot up under the kitchen table, and gave a couple of quick four-hundred-horsepower thrusts to the linoleum.

41

This was all back long ago, and of course nothing could be done about it now. It was really more Alford's story than it was theirs anyway, more the last story about that old, old man than anything else.

Over the breakers, beyond the pier and far out to sea a ship moved slowly on the horizon, as if it were pulled along by the force of their eyes leading it. It moved with them as they walked along the beach. They had been to see Mitchell's brother in Fort Worth, and now they were at the Gulf for the last few days of their trip. They would have to go home soon.

"Look," she says, pointing out along the wooden pier, "a sea gull standing on the piling just like in the brochures."

"Yes," he says, "I see it."

Mitchell let go of her arm and bent over to pick up a broken shell. "Look at this one."

"Yes," she says, "you must have a whole pocketful by now."

"Not too many."

They walked past a man boiling clams without looking at him, and then up a few steps to the wooden planking of the pier. The pier struck out silently into the ocean. A few shacks were pitched along one side of it, and light poles were placed at intervals. It was late in the afternoon and only a few other people were there—a few fishermen, a man selling bait. As they walked they looked through the cracks between the planks down into the ocean. They nearly bumped into a man carrying the largest fishing rod Mitchell had ever seen. The man said, "How do you do," to them in the gruffest and kindest voice they had ever heard.

They both said, "Fine, thank you," and moved over to one side.

The gruff man walked away.

He made them wonder.

At one of the little weather-beaten shacks out on the pier Mitchell rented a fishing rod and bought some bait.

"What is this?"

"Shrimp."

"I wanted some fishing bait."

"Right," the bait man said.

"Oh."

Jenny gave Mitchell a look with her mouth open. "I am fifty-seven years old and didn't know you don't use worms to fish in the ocean," he said. They went out to the very end of the pier and sat down. It was very hot in the afternoon and not a good time to fish. But they had hats and a free afternoon.

Mitchell put a shrimp on the hook and said, "Look how heavy the weight is."

"That's so the ocean won't move your line."

"I guess so."

The ocean was a good twenty feet below them, and then it was only fifteen feet or so. And then it was twenty feet again and they could see barnacles on the pilings where the ocean usually was. Mitchell dropped his hook into the water and let the line reel out. It stopped dropping after a while and he clicked the reel over to make the line taut. He couldn't believe it, but he thought he might have a fish already—the line was so heavy and the tip of the rod bent. He reeled in very

146

quickly till the weight and hook cleared the surface. Then he and Jenny bent far over their knees, out over the ocean, and looked down. No fish.

"Just a heavy weight, I guess," said Mitchell, and he dropped the line back down into the water. Jenny took half a sandwich out of her pocket, broke it up in pieces and cast it on the water for the gulls.

Still the water rose and fell below them. It had since they had been there, a day and a half. She said, "The ocean lasts a long time, doesn't it."

"Forever," Mitchell said, as if he had just read it in a pamphlet.

"I had no idea," she added, glancing down and grinning.

Mitchell leaned over and looked at his line and raised back up smiling. "Look," he says, "I'm fishing in the ocean."

"It's like watching the creek back home, watching the waves; you can watch them all day."

"Water's water," he told her.

They sat there quietly for a few minutes, till Mitchell grew restless again and reeled in his line. The bait was gone.

"Look at that; stole my bait."

"Maybe you didn't put it on right."

"I think I did it right. I don't know. I watched a guy back there."

Jenny glanced back over her shoulder at the continent of North America. "It's a long way home."

"Not so far. The Quirks Run empties into this very ocean, comes this far probably every couple of days. Old Alford, God, the things he used to tell me, all out of breath."

"That was all such a long time ago," she said, and swung her foot out and back in, mimicking the movement of the waves. Mitchell had rebaited, dropped the line in and was already reeling it in again. They leaned out over their shoes. The bait was gone again, and the gold hook gleamed in the sun setting over the western edge of the earth. Mitchell baited the hook and instead of dropping the line straight down next to the pier, cast it toward South America.

That seemed to satisfy him greatly and he sat back down on the pier's edge. He said, "But sometimes I think maybe I could have saved the old guy."

Jenny ran her hands along her dress and onto the gray boards of the pier. "No, no you couldn't have. I didn't let you try."

"Well, I think it less the older I get." He reeled in the line and found the bait hanging limply from the end of the hook. He put another shrimp on and dropped the line back down into the sea.

"You were right. It was just at the time . . . him, and him knowing Dad; I hated to let him go."

"I know."

"My gosh," Mitchell said.

"It was his decision. He made up his mind."

Mitchell clicked the reel over when he felt the weight on the bottom and handed it to Jenny. He said, "I don't fault you. I don't fault anyone, not any more." He got up and brushed off his pants. "I'll go get us something to eat. We can sit here all evening." He started to walk away but turned after a few steps. She was watching him. He turned with his arms spread, "'Cause I feel the old guy here, I feel him and Dad in lots of places; everywhere seems like home. I don't fault no one, no more." Then he walked away, down the pier.

She turned back around and slightly lifted the end of the fishing rod. It bumped secretly in her hand. And so she did what Mitchell had been doing all afternoon—the suspense was almost unbearable—she turned the crank on the reel slowly, lifting the line up from the bottom of the very sea.

This was the story: It was the spring of 1948, fifteen years ago. The rains had been heavy for a week, and the Mus-katatuck was on the rise. It was just a few feet from the back porch of John Alford's house. Trees and debris floated along the muddy bank. There were eight of them there to help: Mitchell, Jenny, Alford, and a few other men, to help turn the old man's house back around facing the river, and more than that: simply to save it. He had lived in the cabin facing uphill since the last flood in '36. The men tied cables to both sides of the old house. They gathered fifty-gallon barrels and tied them under the wooden foundation. It was a great adventure. The rain came all day long; the river crept under the house and lifted it gently. The cables held stout. They all gathered down the bank, where the house would come to its new resting spot after the cables were cut on the upstream side of the house and it caught in the current and swung around. Everyone was shouting and laughing, safely up-hill. And then there was a splash. The old man was in the river, swimming toward an uprooted tree floating down the river. All of the men moved along the bank, shouting. Mitchell took half a step toward the river and found him-self sprawling in the mud. He tried to get up but couldn't. He looked back at his feet. Jenny was crying, covered in mud, holding on to his legs with all of her weight.

"Dammit, let go."

"No!" she screamed. "Don't."

He put his boot on her shoulder and shoved her away, scrambling to his feet. He couldn't spot the old man in the muddy water for a moment and ran forward a few steps. Then he saw him far out in the river in the branches of the tree. It was useless. He turned to her.

"Goddammit, Jenny."

They walked along the bank almost absentmindedly. They watched the old man work his way out of the branches till he lay on top of the tree's huge black trunk. And they stood there, watching him, as he swept the hair back out of his eyes, looked back and waved at them. Then he was holding on, grasping the trunk with arms and legs, and craning his neck to see ahead, as he rounded a bend in the swift river, holding on as if he would ride all the way to the ocean, the old ocean, the endearing sea.

42

About ten miles out of town on the Decatur Road, where the Portersville Pike crosses it, there is a small fruit and vegetable stand. A smooth-skinned, fleshy woman, about forty-five, runs the stand, and has for fifteen or twenty years. She is short, only five feet one, laughs constantly, and has tight little balled-up cheeks close to her nose that resemble plums. She works a two-acre garden to keep the stand supplied, and has twenty fine plum trees. Plums, her name and her passion. Plums lives in a small trailer that was originally designed as a vacation trailer, to be towed behind a car. She bought it new and had it installed behind her stand. At night her television set gives the trailer a warm, eerie glow, and you can tell by the way the trailer shifts which end Plums happens to be in.

Along with her vegetables and fruit, Plums makes and sells her own jelly and jam: Plum Cherry, Plum Grape, Plum Orange, Plum Peach, Plum Cinnamon, and, as a joke, Plum Plum and Plum Crazy. It always tickles her to look at the Plum Crazy labels, and to look at the expressions of first-time customers when they spy the labels. She always thought her wants were simple and fulfilled. She has built up a reputable, successful business. She owns her trailer, her stand, and the ground they sit on. She almost always seems to be happy.

But this is something else, a thing that happened only a few months ago. And aren't our motives for our strangest acts, when we discover them, at times so very uninteresting and trivial? This is offered in compensation and consolation. Because no one yet knows what Plums' motive or motives were. There is speculation, of course. That she was lonely, born of gypsies, or simply crazy, like the jelly. But only speculation. She is still there, in her stand, ten miles out on the Decatur Road; perhaps you can stop by for an ear of corn and plumb her yourself.

He was a big man, with the conventional black leather jacket and swastikas. His girl hung on him like the jacket. She was a little thing who seemed to pout constantly. They pulled up in front of Plums' stand, the motorcycle idling loudly, blat-blat-blat-blat. Plum-blat-could-blat-hardly-blat-hear-blat-herself-blat-think. The girl sat on the bike while the man, bearded and careless, sacked up a few apples and peaches. Plums said, "That will be sixty-three cents, please. Care to try some jelly?"

The man didn't even look up, but gave the sack of fruit to the girl, who squealed. Plums began to worry. There was no one else at the stand. After he had bruised a few tomatoes, she gathered the courage to speak again: "That will be sixty-three cents, please."

"Okay," he said, "give me the sixty-three cents, then, Fatty." He looked at her and smiled. "And any other cents you've got back there." He thrust out his oily hand.

Before she could stop herself, Plums picked up a pear and heaved it at the man. It struck him on the chest. At first it seemed he would tear the stand apart, but then he caught the eye of the girl on the bike, and acted as if the pear had disastrously wounded him. He sprawled on his back in front of the stand, laughing hysterically, screaming in mock pain. Plums caught him glancing up at the girl, and, taking the opportunity, flipped a watermelon off the edge of the stand. It landed roundly on the man's groin. Suddenly the shrieks were much more piercing. The girl on the bike jumped down to help him, but seemed embarrassed, of all things, to touch the man, who was rolling in the gravel in front of the stand and screeching. Finally, the girl helped him onto the back of the big Harley-Davidson, sidesaddle. Then she got on and prepared to drive off. Plums' sack of fruit lay scattered on the ground.

And this is the part no one can comprehend. Plums suddenly became overwhelmed with fear and possibility. Possibility won out. She ran around the stand as fast as her short, thick legs could carry her. She shoved the man off the bike, and boxed the ears of the girl. She got on the bike. The man tried to get up and she backed him down by aiming a peach at his groin. She grabbed the girl by her bra, grabbing it in front and twisting it, and ordered her to tell how the bike worked. The girl spit out everything she knew. Plums stalled the machine twice, but then she did two frightening doughnuts in the gravel and roared off down the Decatur Road. The girl and road thug sat in the gravel and cursed and cried.

The handlebars of the bike were raised up very high, and Plums could only barely see over them. But she roared through Decatur, and finally got the handling of the big machine down so she could relax a little. She watched the road go under her wheels and the countryside slip by. Her hair blew in the wind. And then, four miles out of Lexington, after a few hours on the open road, she realized that this was not the life for her, and turned the big road machine around.

43

Harvest haze, heat, September now, even the bugs are tired. The world is old and fat, tomatoes are splitting, a breath of wind makes a cornfield scream, everything is going hard or soft. The earth ripens to rot, and they move along the rows, the old man and woman, trying to catch the earth on the verge.

"Imagine," he says, or not even having to imagine, because it was true; just accept was what he meant, "imagine: the whole land, the sweep, breadth of it, bursting right this very moment and people scattered all over it, bending over or knees in the earth trying to gather it up, the excess, the spoil and loot of it, cutting and stacking and stripping, sacking, bunching, baling, and busheling, canning. Imagine," he says, meaning accept, "the apples of Maine and the corn of Iowa, some old fellow eating grapes out of a tub in California, an even older one plucking raspberries in Ohio, some lean Texan waiting on the first pecan to drop out of his trees into his palm. Imagine," he says, leaning around and avoiding accept, "the folks baling hay in Wyoming, and a big fat woman eating a grapefruit right off the tree in Florida, the fellow in the next field cutting tobacco, and Jesus, I almost forgot, the little guys in China knee-deep in rice, the Russians growing whatever in the hell they grow, caviar and rotten potatoes, and oh yes, the slack-jawed Idaho guy with his potatoes, and the French guy with his big ol' red grapes, they're all monks—the guys, not the grapes—the Dutch guy with his cow full of milk, and the English, they must grow peat, oh can you just imagine (meaning accept) it all."

Jenny straightens up, the tobacco knife in one hand, the spear in the other, and stares into the sun. "I am just trying to focus in on this one acre. It gets bigger every year. I think you are talking too much and not doing your share of the work."

"It is the harvest, the straw thing full of fruits and vegetables, the time of plenty, and we are right in the midst of it," he yodels, knifing down a six-foot broad-leaf plant, swinging it around to the horizontal and splitting its three-inch trunk over the metal spear, down onto the thin tobacco stick. There were five plants on the stick now, so he took the spear off the stick and moved down the row. He put the sharp steel spear on another stick and drove the other end of the stick into the ground. Now he was ready to cut again. They worked two rows at a time, cutting, spearing. It was hard, hot work, and it came at the hottest time of the year, September dog days. It was dangerous too. A knife, shaped like a razor-bladed hatchet, could cut a toe off as easily as a tobacco plant. A slip trying to jam a stalk over the spear could be a lost eye. And after the tobacco was cut, it was loaded on wagons and taken to the barn and hung to cure. And hanging the tobacco, placing it on poles high in the rafters of the barn, killed men every year. Mitchell had broken an arm in a fall once.

"So imagine beyond that even," he says, (meaning so accept beyond that even), knifing the tobacco, sweat dropping off his brow to the earth, "the . . ."

"How do you feel? How is your stomach?" she says.

"It's fine. I'm fine. It's been six months since our operations. I'm fine. How are you? Your two gallstones gone."

"Fine. I can work. Fine."

"So imagine beyond that even," he insists, "the years, the timeless ancient harvest, the endless autumns, the harvest homes, the bins of grain, the sacks of onions, the

154

bushels of wheat, grown by my father and all our fathers —the old Kentuckians, the New Englanders, the peasants and serfs and slaves, growing their good souls to feed the king, all the way back to that old, old Assyrian with his hoe of stone. Imagine," he goes and goes, meaning accept, "the harvests and harvest times beyond that, that the forests and the meadows knew, and they in turn known by the deer and the rabbit and the brontosaurus. The harvests, the good times. Food. Imagine."

"Yes," she says, "all right, all right. I can see it all. I am imagining, all right."

"Then," he says, "go on, imagine beyond that and all other things and imagine us not here, imagine the whole world, all the other bent backs and elbows going on as if we were not here, as it has gone on since who knows when. Imagine us not here, not doing our part and the world and time going on without us. Imagine that."

"Why?"

"Imagine that."

"How are you?" she asks, standing up, wiping away the sweat. "How is your stomach? Do you feel the part missing?"

"The tumor? It's gone and I'm fine. Like you and your stones of all the gall."

"You think about this," she says, "you think of us standing in the middle of this harvest in this field, standing and working in it right now, and no one else, just us. That you have done it all your life, and this is you, and you are doing it now."

"Yes," he says, "I have accepted that."

"All right then," she relents.

"But the other," he says, "we must imagine that. Your two stones, like little green peas, and me, my tumor, 'about the size of a healthy peach,' the doctor said, placing it in a jar: our personal harvests this year."

155

44

To be broken down on the American highway nine miles out of town is a miserable thing. If there are two of you, here is what you say after the inevitable, inexorable clanking and stall of the car, after you have let it roll as far as it will down the gravel shoulder, and the primitive and awful possibility of having to walk nine miles bears down upon you:

"What in the hell do you suppose that was?"

"Does it look like I'm out there under the hood?"

"All right, all right, let's get out and look."

"You and your damn cars. You never put a drop of oil or water or grease in 'em. No wonder we're broke down here."

"You wanted a ride, didn't you? You can walk from here on in. I ain't stopping you."

"My God, it must be a hundred degrees. I ain't walking nowhere. You promised a ride."

"Well, you're going to have to walk down to that creek down there and get some water. I think it's hot. Take this pop bottle."

"My God, I'll have to make a hundred trips."

"It's all we got."

"See, that wasn't so bad. Why is it only half full?"

"I had to have a drink. Long way up from that creek."

"Well, all right. I don't think it's hot anyway."

"What is it?"

"Look at that."

"Geeo."

"I'll never buy another damn Hudson long as I live."

"Why would they make that part so hard to get to?"

"So you'd have to pay them to work on it. Make 'em so they'll break fast too. All them car makers do."

"How could a part rust that much in just sixteen years?"

"Cheap Japanese steel."

"Oh, I better get some rocks to chock the wheels. This thing's starting to roll."

"Disaster's always at hand. I can fix that rust, though. Let me get my tools. I got some stuff in a spray can here that automatically dissolves all rust and corrosion."

"Don't spray that stuff on too heavy. Might not have much of a car left. Well. You got it. Don't bugger up the threads now."

"Give me that hammer."

"Careful."

"Son of a bitch. You knew that was coming, didn't you?"

"I said careful. I saw some baling wire down there on the hill. We can tie that part there down. It'll hold."

"Okay."

"That bolt there is too long."

"That's all right. I've got seven or eight washers in the toolbox."

"You broke that cotter pin, didn't you? Here's a nail."

"Could you siphon a little gas out of the tank and we'll prime this carb."

"Here's the gas. I found some of Irene's Noxzema in the back seat. Grease up that shaft with it."

"Good idea. I used some of your duct tape to wrap around that hose. That will hold it for a while."

"Look at them globs of white stuff on the battery terminals."

"Yeah, better clean them off."

"Whoops. Shit. Blew a fuse doing that, I bet."

"You scared me to death. Careful with those cables. You'll shock the hell out of yourself."

"Yep, blew a fuse."

"Here's a Wrigley's wrapper. Wrap the foil around there and put it back in."

"Jesus, it's a hundred degrees if it's ten."

"All right, hit the starter for me. . . . Are you hitting it?"

"Do you see this baseball bat in my hand?"

"All right, wait a minute. Battery's dead."

"What are you . . . why are you climbing up on the bumper . . . my God, what are you peeing on the battery for?"

"I'm peeing in the battery. Give it a little extra shot of power."

"My God, is it worth it?"

"Okay, try it now."

"Okay, here goes."

"Hey, hey, hey, listen to that. Don't let her die now."

"No, sir."

"Here now, let me get my toe on the accelerator and you scoot over. There. Listen to her purr, would you."

"Like brand-new."

"These old Hudsons ain't bad cars. Stout cars. You can work on 'em. You seen them new '64 models. So much under the hood you can't see the engine."

"Wouldn't have one."

"Yes, sir. We're on easy street, back on the road again."

45

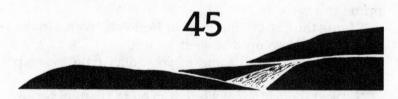

"Mr. Parks, we're going to let you rent."

Out in the street in front of the bank he was able to let the concentration go, but the muscles of his face held taut. So, not only the adjoining property gone, but the home farm lost too. Across the street a banner was slung across

a car dealership window, 1937—YOUR YEAR FOR A ROAD-
STER. He turned and headed out of town back up the
Decatur Road. He would rent now.

"That's wonderful," she said, leaning out over the thick
kitchen table, "we can stay then?"
"If we can pay the rent," he said, leaning back in his
chair, his hands in his lap.
"It's a smaller payment. We'll have money left over."
And she pushed the salt and pepper shakers around the
table. She couldn't hide her relief.
"I think so."
"At least we won't be out on the road, Mitchell. You'll
still be around this place. No one else will be on it."
"I know it."

And he was there in the field, plowing, going through
what he thought were somehow the saddest and most
basic of motions, when the first squadron of silver bomb-
ers flew over, fresh from the plant in Lexington. He felt
the fear and hope and longing of the world go through
him. And it only required two years, twenty-four quick
months, to get the economy boiling, to get people to pay
time and again what tobacco and pigs and goats were
worth.

Out of the sun and into the cool darkness of the bank. A
new loan officer.
"Glad to meet you, Mr. Parks. So you want to become
a landowner. Well. Mr. Parks, do you own a tractor? Mr.
Parks, you could sell that mule, and with what you have
pay half down on a fine tractor, and I'd be more than
happy to write you a credit sheet on the other half. I've
already written up tractor loans for a dozen farmers. The
war is going to require a huge output, and to keep up
we're all going to have to mechanize. I can hold that

159

property you rent. I don't think anyone else is going to want to purchase it. After you've got the tractor paid off, then you can put a down payment on that farm. All right then, just trying to help with a little sound business sense. Here's your schedule. You'll own the farm in twenty-five years. Time enough to give it to the grandchildren, eh?"

He would stand up, in 1946 or '57 or '63, lean back on his hoe, and count the rows he still had to work. Then he would look to see where the sun was.

It was very bright inside the renovated bank, and warm; the air-conditioning had broken down. A new loan officer. "Last payment. Bet you're glad of that. How does it feel to own your own land, lock, stock and barrel? Mr. Parks, there is a fine piece of property that backs right up to your place."

The deed, the little yellow paper in the center of the old kitchen table (thick and scarred and burned, the table) held all their attention. They were very tired. Mitchell pushed his hat back up on his head, revealing, above the tan line, a block of porcelain forehead. They walked out on the porch and saw, surprisingly, that the land and the day looked very much like it did the day before. Jenny rubbed Mitchell's back, then her own. Mitchell sent a black ball of coal spit scudding along the warp of a porch board and said, "I'll write Brice and Stilman and let them know. They'll get a kick out of it."

Dear Brother,
How in the cat's hair are you all anyway? We are all fine as frog's teeth. You can show this letter to all your friends to prove you've got real hillbilly relatives. ha ha.
Well, it is late September now and I have just been down to the bank in Decatur to pay off the note on the farm. Every square foot of it is ours again, and I guess Dad

can roll back over in his grave and finally get some rest. It feels oh so good I can't tell you. I have spent my whole life reaccomplishing what Dad accomplished. It is a sad case to put before the judge. I worked four good mules literally into the ground. The real irony of the situation is that we never needed that piece of property adjoining the farm. None of my boys cared a lick about farming, and none of the girls married farmers. So it is all like one big joke played on me. It was hard to laugh for a while but I can now.

Jenny has put the deed in the metal box and it is safe. If I have any regrets about the farm it is because of her. She is the only person I know who has a better soul than old Zeke. We will never put a mortgage on this place again. Unless, I guess, one of the kids gets into trouble. And then it wouldn't bother me.

Well, I have just got me a new grandbaby, born to Stephen and his wife up in New York. Jenny and I have pictures but haven't seen him yet. I guess we could get up and leave anytime now and stay away as long as we wanted. The farm will always be here, only the taxes to pay now every year.

Well, I have to go. This letter writing cramps your hand. It seems like the ol' US of A is good again today. The farm is ours. I sure would like to see you soon.

Mitchell

46

Deserted buildings draw as many people as they do rats. About eight miles out from town where two cross-pikes join the Decatur Road and make a curious peace symbol

out in the middle of nowhere, there is a good-sized building in a cornfield. You have to climb over a fence and
walk across the corn stubble to get to it. It's a pretty neat
old building at first: tile roof and stone walls. But then
you see all of the windows have been broken out and
the whole thing is about to fall in. Just inside the front
door somebody has dug a big hole in the floor. You
find yourself in a big room, but some farmer has got
it full of hay. Some of it's green hay and might burn
if the guy's not careful. Over in the corner there is a
roll of loose baling wire and some old chairs that look
like they used to be bolted down in a ship. No telling
what the place used to be, out here in the middle of
nowhere.

On the other side of the place there are just mounds
and mounds of broken glass and mirrors. And more hay.
You can see the rabbits and rats have been having a
time. Droppings everywhere. The thing is to be on the
lookout for some antique. Something neat you could
clean up and put on the living-room wall. This place was
probably cleaned out a dozen years ago, though. Bunch
of junk. Over on this side there is a lot of tile, worn right
through to the foundation. You can tell at this one spot
that something heavy must have sat there. The tiles are
dented but not worn. More chairs in the corner. A roll of
barbed wire. A bunch of old red restaurant booths, all
ripped up. Junk.

There's a big back porch to the place. There's something. An old yellow wrought-iron bench. Nailed to the
floor. Couldn't get it up with a tank. And then you can
see what this place used to be. Down on the ground,
below the porch, is an old railroad bed. The rails are
gone but a few of the ties are still there, tumbled and
rotten. Used to be an old railroad station. Christ, you
think, all the people that went through this place. Just a
dump now, though.

47

The dishes were done, her hands still pink and wrinkled from the hot water. The pink would go in a few minutes, but most of the wrinkles would stay; they weren't the water's fault at all. Weren't the water's fault.

From far back in their bedroom a song came floating through the door and around a corner. It hung like a shaft of poor light in the front room and then passed through the gauze curtains out onto the front porch. She was there, on the swing, waiting. It was an old phonograph and record, and if she got far enough away the pops and cracks would drop out of the song—fall on her bed, into the crevices of the rope rug in the front room, and the last few scratches must catch in the sheer curtains. It was a sad song, low and slow and far away, like the hum of silence after a bird chirps only once.

Oh, the fall. Autumn was almost here. The last dust of September had filtered down to earth. The dusk showed it most. The sun would just give up and a little wind would slip out of the hills and come cautiously tree-to-tree down the knobsides, stop before it confronted the heat and bulk of the house, get nervous and back off. The past was hidden in dusk. It was folded up like an old blue quilt. The fall was almost here.

She looked up on the ridge and saw that the moon was rising into the feathers of the day. A harvest moon, round and orange. It held there faint and small at first, wavering in the heat off the pines and firs on the ridgetop, then the day backed off like some shy, understanding old man, and the moon rose and unfurled as if she were in

163

a ball dress and had just been asked to dance. Silliness.

The song fell away, and she was left there alone with the porch and the night and the cautious wind, the last of September. A cluster of gnats hung in the air above her. They looked like a diagram of some complicated atom, whispering around in a weird devotion to an unseen center. She watched the gnats till they came too close and she fanned them away, splitting the atom. She had eaten enough gnats in her day. Her hands had lost the pink color and even a few of the wrinkles.

She turned back and the moon was still there. Men, not just a man, had walked there this summer. Had actually jumped up and down on the surface of the moon. Walter Cronkite had said, in the most honest piece of journalism she had ever heard, "Oh boy, oh boy, oh boy . . ." It was amazing and somehow irritating, that they had done it, gotten to that old old inaccessible place. People were always wanting to go somewhere. Mitchell had always wanted to go, just go, and the children had, every last one of them. This was home here. She would never understand it. And what were they bothering the moon for? They knew what was up there. It was a violation of something, somewhere.

The night. She had always thought herself so mysterious because she loved the night. There were unknown things there, all safe and kind, at the worst mischievous, and she thought she was one of them. There were the ones, not elves or fairies or anything as simple as that, but the ones who rustle in the night, who stare itches into the small of your back while you change the flat tire on the lonely road, ones who work to carry small animals across busy roads, ones who snatch frogs from the night and place them in the most remarkable places—on the roof, in a tree. Just what she was in charge of, or responsible for, she didn't know. Perhaps it was the clashing of pots and pans under the kitchen sink when all were in bed. Silliness.

She got up from the porch swing and walked back through the house. Mitchell was already in bed, early for him. The fan blew gently over him, pushing at the sheets, trying to cover him up. She remembered far back and far away, beyond the night and the song, farther away even than the harvest moon. She had sat on the corner of this bed night after night, waiting for Mitchell to finish with his work and come in. The fan blew across her face, cool and sudden. She had wanted to be a poet, or to live like a poet, and had no notion as to how to go about it. She reached over and turned out the bed lamp, and the night came through the open window and filled the room. She had felt, on those long-ago nights, a complete mystery to herself, simply because she was young and couldn't already look back on her whole life. She had been unsure of everything, even of Mitchell, and so she had remained, as long as possible, inaccessible. But things were different now. She was sixty, and what was ahead wouldn't be much different from what had passed. She looked for the moon outside the window; it was gone, and there were only stars. But he had gotten to her. She had always known that he needed her, anyone who saw him walk down the road could see that he needed somebody. He was even snoring now. She pushed him over. And well, he had wanted her too, after all. Here he was. That was a long time ago.

Oh, the night. Oh, the moon. They had reached it at last. And she felt that something was lost. Some old mystery. All this time passed by. She could look back on it all. She had, as she could see it, two options: she could push herself farther into the night, beyond the moon, beyond Mars and Saturn, to some distant point of light, and then turn around to face the earth, to live the new life and wait for whatever would occur. Or she could simply not believe Walter Cronkite. It was all a big patriotic hoax. Who said those rocks were moon rocks? Well, either option would work. It was late. And work to do tomorrow.

165

She lay back in the bed next to Mitchell. Silliness. An old woman's silliness. The night. He really had wanted her, and had all this time. Silliness. She could not repeat the same words in that tone. She was an old woman who was not silly. Walter Cronkite. So she let this suffice: She pulled the pillow back under her head and spoke in the most proper, sleepy, serious demeanor, "Oh, boy."

48

You have ordered and eaten your Harvest Hamburger at the first hamburger stand on the road to Decatur. The waitress, soft-soled, asks you for the second time if there is anything else. Lord, you wonder, looking up into her amazing green eyes, how can you tell her that there is plenty else, everything else? The world is melancholy, like an old wooden chair in the attic, in autumn, at dusk, when the hamburger's eaten and the most beautiful green eyes in the world ask if there is anything else. How can you tell her you love her more than anything else on earth? You say you would like just to sit at the counter for a while and read "The Story of the Hamburger" on the back of the menu. She says, "Sure," and you look for a smile, but there is none. She is dusk itself. Who sired and birthed her? Who wrote her? Will there never be an end to these questions?

So you read the hamburger story and find, beyond all expectations, that a hamburger's story is an interesting one: American-born, its separate parts may come from ten different states. It is a symbol of America itself. You are so proud.

Over in the corner old Dean Moriarty broods over a cup

of java. Dig him. He must be, what? Forty-four or -five, now? He looks beat, worn. He winks at the old lady behind the cash register as you pay and walk out. God love his heart.

Autumn dusk. The ground is withered melon vine and corn stubble, dry and skeletal, like bird bones broadcast over the fields. Old Moriarty comes out of the hamburger stand and you let him bum your last four bits. He smiles. He skips over to a new Cadillac and roars off down the Decatur Road. You are standing there in the gravel of the parking lot, watching him go. That son of a bitch.

So you walk on down the road. A few cars already have their lights on. A meadowlark glides low over the stubblefields. You lose the bird in the dusk. Down the road a few yards an old man is burning a pile of fallen leaves. Won't it be nice to smell the smoke from those leaves? So you walk on down the road a bit faster, but then something flutters and stalls in your mind. Some old wild promise or hope. The green-eyed waitress! You didn't say goodbye, or even look at her one last time. You stop on the road to Decatur. In that moment of indecision is every story ever told. And you decide, standing there on the edge of the asphalt, that every dilemma is at last this one: choosing between an old man standing over smoking leaves, and a green-eyed waitress who doesn't even smile when she says, "Sure."

49

The windfall: He had been to the doctor over fifteen times for checkups and visited the government offices so much that he knew the number of curls in the bangs of the receptionist there. And nothing had come of it. And so when the black-lung check came, $17,839.42, it was a big thing. The letter said $17,839.42 in back payments, and $350 per month from this date forward. He promptly wrote four one-thousand dollar checks and sent one to each of the children. Jenny bought new living-room furniture. The winters in the coal mines had finally paid off. He could really still breathe pretty well yet.

50

Joe Smith has it all figured out. He used to work seven or eight different roads. He used to walk twenty, twenty-five miles a day picking up aluminum cans. But that is all past now; he has it all figured out; all of those years of walking miles and miles are over; it is almost as if Joe were retired. Instead of all of that walking he simply works a mile section of the Decatur Road: the mile that immediately follows the road sign that says it's five more miles to Decatur. It was peculiar. He came upon this section of the Decatur Road last fall and knew, then and there, that he could make his life's living off that one stretch of asphalt. The Decatur Road is like the trunk of a great tree of roads branching out into the mountains. People would come down out of the hills, off a twig to a limb, to the Decatur Road. They would drink their pop on their way to Decatur. And then, when they saw the five-mile sign, a sudden impulse to clean out the car would overcome them. Out the window went the cans. And for the past year Joe Smith has been there on the side of the road with his burlap bag catching cans.

Well, this is about all. Other than the fact that Joe Smith can chew a wad of tinfoil without going into convulsions, he is a completely unremarkable person. Even if you were a writer you would find nothing else interesting to say about him.

51

For the last few years he had been killing his hogs in early fall. Before that he had had to wait for the first freeze, but now he had a big stand-up freezer. He could dress out a hog anytime now, but waited for the fall to avoid the flies and heat of summer. He had two big cast-iron caldrons set up on a special brick stand. A fire burned beneath them and the water in the pots was beginning to boil. The hot water, when poured on the pig's skin, would loosen the hair. A good metal scraper would take it off fairly easily then.

Dragging the carcass was a one-man job with a winch. Mitchell had the line looped over a stout locust limb so he could lift the hog up in the air for gutting and butchering. He had sharpened all of his knives the night before and now they lay sparkling on the grass.

His rifle was propped up against the trunk of the old tree. He had killed—how many?—a hundred hogs, maybe, under this tree. The blue steel of the gun's barrel glowed dully in the morning's cool sun. He picked up the rifle, leaned over the board railing of the pigsty. The big hog was nervous. He trotted stiffly to a corner, turned, glanced at Mitchell, trotted to the far corner, and then repeated the pattern. Mitchell set the rifle on the fence and aimed into the corner where the pig turned and eyed him. He would shoot him cleanly between the eyes when the pig looked at him as he turned. The pig reached the far corner, turned and trotted joltingly back to the near corner. It would be a shot of only a few feet. The pig reached the corner. He turned, lifted his snout at Mitchell, and looked at him.

How many times in a man's life does he start to kill something and then stop himself at the last moment? And what is it that makes him have the queerest sense of shame afterward? The starting or the stopping? And why do old men feel the slightest things so intensely?

These things might pass through his mind: That he no longer needs to kill, that at one time it was necessary and respectable, but now is neither. That a man, if he could see in front of himself, would realize that in a hundred or two hundred years, meat-eating would be in the same class as incest and slavery. He might look down the barrel of his rifle back to that old admonishment, that man's meat is the fruit of the land. He might consent that a man's teeth and guts weren't designed for or haven't adapted to meat. He might see that all life is sacred, not just human life, and that the only inalienable rights were the rights to life, however degrading or miserable or unfulfilled. That a pig is no different from any dog, any man. And he might remember the story from Vietnam, of a man who was trained to live and fight with his dog, who was saved by him, slept and ate with him, and had to kill him when the war was over and he had to go home, the dog unable to live alone. And how the man cried. And this pig's life no different from that dog's or that man's. He might understand that it was the noun, "life," that counted, and not the modifier, the adjective, "man's," "pig's," "dog's." These things might be plain to him when it comes to pulling the trigger.

And if he is not just a man but an old man pulling the trigger, it may not be the pig's life at all, not at all, but something more universal and personal than rights even: death and his own death. And he might become nervous or even afraid on the sudden, the crosshairs of the sight dipping up and down. He confronts death as the end of all things and then decides to face and accept it or ignore it, rationalize it. If he does the first, he doesn't shoot, that is, if he's not an angry or psychopathic person. If he does the second, it doesn't matter if he shoots or not.

He might see that the only thing that matters is to come out of this thing with a little bit of respect. And being an old man, he understands that he can do without the death of one more pig. That he can eat beans. He might stand up and leave the pig, let him out of the sty, turn the caldrons of hot water into the fire, put the sharpened knives into scabbards. Realize that, to those who love and enjoy life, death is a horrible thing. Why deny it? To cry out at death is the most honorable thing.

Perhaps as he sights between the pig's eyes, all these things pass through his mind.

Or, maybe, more likely, none of these things occur to him and he kills without a moment's hesitation, simply out of habit, with murder still an acceptable form of, not survival, but luxury.

How do you understand an old man?

52

The blood in the killing room was several inches deep. The floor drain must have been clogged again. It was break time. The men sat on the benches in the corner of the room, drinking coffee. The coffee machine was up on a table. The blood couldn't get to it.

"We will set us a record today, I bet you." The man reached up and shifted his suspenders. The hip-waders the men wore were heavy and caused the suspenders to dig into their shoulders.

"I never saw such a sheepish bunch of steers," another man said. "Must have all been raised on molasses in the hot sun."

"Sure kill faster. Easy killed. They walk right up to you." All of the men were talking now.

"We'll set a daily record for sure. Maybe even break an hourly. We can really hit it after the break. Get that record bonus."

"Think they'd give it?" the youngest man asked.

"Better."

"Better."

"Somebody unclog that drain. Can't work in this stuff." The man who had been at it the longest dipped his coffee cup into the warm morning's blood. He took a sip, as if it would scorch his tongue. Two of the men turned away from him.

"Christ, how can you do that?"

"It's good," the man said, "keeps you healthy, puts hair on your chest."

"Christ."

A man who had not spoken said, "We got to kill a hundred and forty-two in an hour. I heard Charley say we can't tie the record and get the money. Got to kill one-forty-two."

"We can do that. Just takes a good crew."

"Sure."

"Won't be no problem if we can get the boys outside to keep 'em coming in."

"They'll do that. They know the record's on the line."

"They can do it."

"We'll have to make sure the guns have new cartridges in them. Don't want to run out of shells after seventy or so."

"I'll slap some in right now." All of the men were talking now.

"What say we switch jobs on the half hour instead of the hour? Me and Jerry and Steve will shoot for the first half hour and then we'll cut. You guys'll cut, then shoot. That way the shooters won't get tired and start missing, having to use two shells instead of one."

"Good idea."

"Will they allow that?"

"Look, it's to their advantage if we set a record. Get more beef through."

"Yeah."

"Yeah."

"I ever tell you guys about killing cattle in Nam? I was in the artillery spotters. We took binoculars up on the hills and spotted targets, radioed them in. If we got bored we'd look for water buffalo in the valleys and call in their coordinates."

"I bet that was hell."

"Not near as much work as this."

"I think it's time, boys."

"Well, let's get that bonus."

"Here you go."

"Okay."

"Y'all ready?"

"Who's keeping time?"

They were all talking now.

"Steve's got it."

"We're ready then."

"Okay, then, Steve."

"On your mark, boys, get set, go."

From the Swanson meat-packing plant it is two and a half miles into Decatur. You can't hear the cattle in Decatur even on cool October nights.

or,

Today a very good lot of beef was in and perhaps a very good job could be done and a record set today.

53

Tobacco is a Christian crop. The markets open up a month or two before the end of the year, and a hundred thousand bleak-looking Christmases in the Virginias and Carolinas, Tennessee and Kentucky are saved by the sale of a good crop. But there is work yet before it goes to the warehouse. It has to be brought down out of the barns after it has cured, and brought down only when it is in case, when the leaves are moist all the way through and tender, like a baby's fingernail. It is a problem of timing: waiting for the late-autumn rain, the foggy mornings and misty nights, and working before the big freeze. The leaves don't wait when they're ready and must be worked—stripped off the stalk, graded, and tied in hands of about a pound each. If you work the tobacco when you want to, it will either rot in the barn or burst into dust when you touch it.

It was late in the night, but they had only been working for a few hours. The tobacco had been in case all evening and they had put it off as long as possible for the anniversary. The anniversary was over now, and they both gave a small sigh of relief when they finally got into the small stripping room next to the barn and started. The room was lighted by a pair of fluorescent tubes

174

Mitchell had put in. Their special light made grading the leaves easier work on his and Jenny's eyes. The tobacco was heaped on one end of a twelve-foot table that took up half of the stripping room. An electric heater was under the table. It and the tar paper tacked on the outside of the little wooden building kept them warm enough to work.

Mitchell stood next to the heap of plants, taking them one at a time and stripping off the broad, tan leaves near the base of each stalk. He moved about halfway up the plant ripping off leaves and then tossed it into a small stack next to Jenny down the table. She pulled off the rest of the leaves, smaller and reddish-brown, and then threw the bare spearlike stalk to the far end of the table.

A radio on a shelf above them played country music, and it was very bright and warm inside the little shack, and work was being done.

It had been the anniversary day, the fiftieth, and they had all come: the brother, Brice; and the children, Henry, Becky, Stephen, and Sarah; and their children; the neighbors; the friends. Even Stilman's son had come in from Texas.

She woke up to the banging of pots and pans in the kitchen. Overslept! And this her golden anniversary. Becky and Sarah were already working in the kitchen. She fought her way into a pull-over dress, snagging her elbow in the cloth as she walked through the bedroom door into the kitchen. There was a crowd of people there, and four or five of them asked who had woken Grandma up and said she wouldn't do any work today. She let them sit her at the kitchen table but said, "I'm just like an old car. I have gone a hundred thousand and you've got out to push me a mile."

She saw Mitchell after a moment, sitting there at the

175

table too, looking around in a state of complete bewilderment. He had his hands out on the table, palms up, as if someone were about to give him something. His hands looked strange with nothing in them. She contemplated the number of times she had seen the pink of his palms.

All of the people wandering about were talking to her all at once. She needed to calm down and pick the words and sentences out and understand them.

"Yes, ma'am, I have lost some weight."

"Grandma, can we go pet Barney?"

She dealt with these and then knifed her way through the mesh of arms and legs to the stove. This was her kitchen. They needed her help to find things. She opened a cabinet and took down flour. She pulled several different kinds of pots and pans out from under the sink. More people were coming in the house. She heard the screen door slam three or four times and heard loud talking, but she couldn't see anyone for the bodies all around her. And then the new people were being pushed into her open arms.

"Why, you're a rail, a rail."

"Fifty years. Fifty years. How much time is that?"

"I'm six."

"Grandma really could use some weight."

"How'd you put up with him all these years?"

Mitchell was standing next to her, shaking hands and smiling. She smiled back at the faces leaning into hers and laughed. Mitchell said something about the tobacco being in case. Already wanting to get out of here, she thought. And here was Henry taking a picture. She stood still for a moment, trying not to blink, till Henry told her again to move over next to Dad. She laughed, turned red, and moved over beside Mitchell. He took her hand.

Still more people come in and others are knocking at the door. She opens the front door and there are more faces. But behind them, Lord, would you look at the cars! The people in, hugged, shoved, and seated. Something is burning in the kitchen. Yams. Sarah never could cook a yam. Ben Perry hands her two silver cups, saying he couldn't find anything gold. Everyone laughs. Everyone is standing and talking. They won't sit down. All the grandchildren here at one time, she thinks, and scans the room. A great-grandbaby. One on the way. Brice and his wife. Stilman's wife and boy.

"No one ever figured him out. That Holland. Guy with the dogs, remember him? Left and never seen again."

The food is ready. She is talking but she should be helping with the food. Walk here. Stop. Meet. Meet. Oh. Yes, yes. All this way. Do not cry. It was just that old memory. New memory.

"Oh, I start at my own words sometimes. It's like somebody else puts them in my mouth."

Becky hands her a plateful of food. Can't eat now. Everyone is sitting down now and eating.

The Wizard of Oz is on TV, y'all."

She is telling another old woman about the arthritis in her wrists. It's all she can do at times. If someone knew that you were bearing up to it, it made it easier to bear.

"Oh, she died years ago, years."

She went back into the kitchen and checked the stove. Someone had let the water boil out of a pot and two eggs were sitting on the hot metal. "I knew I'd forget." Everyone is bringing their plates into the kitchen. The girls are washing them. She points. They go here and that goes down there. It is hot in the kitchen. She puts a hand on Henry's shoulder and says, "Oh, this old, worn-out body; I'm sick of it."

"Mom," he says, and she smiles.

They are all talking again, gathered in groups throughout the house.

"No, no more for me, I'm flabbergasted."

"This was so good, Jenny."

"Yes."

Mitchell put another half-stripped stalk on her stack. She took it, stripped off the last few leaves and threw the bare stalk to the end of the table. This went on and on. Mitchell brought in another load of plants from the wagon load outside and then carried out the stack of stripped stalks to a huge pile of them against the shed. When the stripping was finished and the tobacco taken to market and sold, there were still these bare stalks. They would put them on a wagon and then he and Jenny would spread them back over the fields. Mitchell, lean and sharp, a stalk himself, rushed back in the stripping room rubbing his hands. "Colder and colder out there," he says.

After the leaves were stripped, they tied them together in hands. Mitchell packed as many leaf stems in his palm as he could and then used another leaf to tie them all together around their stems. The bunch looked like the matted straw of a witch's broom. When they had made eight or ten hands, they perched them over a tobacco stick and pressed them. It would make for fewer wagon loads to the warehouse.

"Stilman's boy sure looks a lot like him, don't he?" Mitchell said.

"I thought I'd seen a ghost when he walked in the door. Sort of broke my heart for a moment."

"Me too."

Brice opened the stripping-room door and stepped in. "Y'all out here late, aren't you?"

Mitchell said, "It's in case, Brice. Got to get it done."

"Well, give me a stalk or two. I'll bet I can still do it."

Jenny said, "No, you go back in the house, Brice. We can finish up here."

"She's right," Mitchell added, "We have just this little bit here to do. You go in. You'll get all sticky and dirty and have to take a shower. We only got enough hot water for two showers."

"What a front you two can put up. As I recall when we were growing up, we didn't have any hot water at all. But all right, all right." And he stepped back outside and started across the yard. Then he yelled out, "But I'm gonna wait up for you."

"Ol' Brice."

"Yeah."

They are all talking about old people and old happenings.

"I like to think about things."

And then Becky and Henry pushed her and Mitchell into the front room. It was time to cut the cake. Becky pulled all of the gold leaves off the cake and gave one to each of the grandchildren. Then Mitchell took the knife from Henry and put Jenny's hand on top of his and they cut the cake and everyone in the room clapped. A baby girl woke up in the corner. They all wanted a speech and Mitchell looked up and said, "Well, I guess we know now that we've been somewhere," and everyone laughed and said, "Amen" and "Yes, sir." And Mitchell was getting into it now and reached over and picked Jenny up, she with knife and plate in hand, picked her up and kissed her on the mouth. Cheers, laughter, more cheers. Well, I am crying, Jenny thinks. All of these old people. I am crying. She trembles like a leaf.

So everyone gets cake and punch, and somebody makes a remark about the punch, saying they wished Wilson Fellers were still around to spike it. And they all laugh at that. It brings them all up out of their cake and they talk again.

"So it started that simple? Out of the dusk and the dust and the thunder?"

179

"I like the punch the way it is."

"It's all to do with making the ordinary mystical and the mystical ordinary."

"Yes, yes, I've lost some weight."

"Ol' George has got dunlop disease. Belly done lopped over his belt."

"Yes, I'll have another."

They talked and talked. They got up and left, falling out of the front door like the leaves off a tree in a strong wind.

Mitchell said, "Why don't you go on in, I'll finish up here."

She laughed and rubbed her hands. It was the hands that went first when you stripped tobacco. "You'll be on your way soon then?"

"I am always on my way." And he leaned over and kissed her on the bone of her cheek.

"All right."

She put her gloves on and went out into the cold night. Mitchell always liked to finish up, to work a little on his own. He seemed to feel guilty if he didn't get to. So she left. He would be in in a few minutes. She walked across the yard, crunching the gravel on the roadway. She stopped there, on the firm road, and let herself drop sweetly and silently into that old sorrow which was only hers. She lent herself to it only on special days, when the house was full of happiness and bright air. She let a tear drop for her lost child, which no one had reminded her of today. And then she started on again, across the road, that moment of complete bliss and indifference gone. And she thought about the people of the day, the variety of human faces, full and flushed and satisfied. She stopped on the front porch and turned around. She looked up at the ridge, across the bare fields, and then at the thin strip of light coming out of the stripping room. And she remembered the faces.

54

About a mile outside of town a median splits the two lanes of the Decatur Road. There are a few businesses scattered on both sides of the road: a farm-implement company, tractors and bush hogs and hay balers lined up on two acres; a county firehouse; a small airport with a grass runway. There are houses on three-acre plots, new ranch-style houses, motley brick, black roofs, aluminum windows and doors, four square feet of front porch. Out to the side of the houses are new four-wheel-drive pickups, a riding lawnmower, and a little aluminum outbuilding to put the lawnmower in.

You can see Decatur in the distance at last. Church steeples, trees mostly, the limestone courthouse. Part of the town is up on a small hill, where the original fort was supposed to have been. The rest of the town flows down the hillside. You cross a bridge, a muddy brown river below. On the other side is a sign: MUSKATATUCK RIVER. Again! If you'd only had a boat!

At the first old house on the outskirts of Decatur the porch light goes out just as you look at it. The moths that were under it flutter away. Suddenly you are very nervous. What is going on here? Something is missing. Or there is too much to take in. You have forgotten what you have been walking all this way for. You start slapping your pockets. And then you are all right.

55

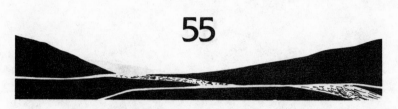

There was the bleakness at first, the long flat oceanlike spread of the days. She would always wake up first and push herself up in the old bed. Then she would look around the room, and out the window. Mitchell would raise up then and she would say, "Put your teeth in, for goodness' sake." And he would do that and then move on to the kitchen to put the coffee on.

There was the bleakness at first, the long flat oceanlike spread of the days. She woke up and pushed herself up. Mitchell woke up too, and said, "What?"

And she said, "I feel real bad."

And he said, "Okay, we'll go to the doctor, right now." And she didn't say anything, so he said, "Well?"

And she said, "Well, I think I'm about to die."

And he said, "Bosh," and felt it somehow inadequate, and said, "bosh," again, softly.

And there was the old bleakness again, the long flat oceanlike spread of the days, when they would both wake up and cry a little.

And there was the bleakness at first, the long flat oceanlike spread of the days. To end with the snap, the arching of her back, in the old bed, when she said, "No," once, very loudly, and "no," once, very softly. There was this in the morning, and for the old man, the rest of that day.

56

Out of place and unexpected, like some extraordinary loophole or last chance, Indian summer squeezes in between autumn and winter during broad daylight, between fog and frost. The last leaves are drifting down on the Decatur Road, on the sidewalks, and on the lawns of the old houses. You take off your sweater and tie it around your neck. The sidewalk is crumbled; the roots of giant maples push up through it. Across the street an old man and woman walk side by side. He steps quickly, gains on the old woman, then stops ten yards ahead and waits for her. This happens again. And again. She is the turtle and he is the hare. How have they stayed together all of these years, walking this way? Was it her perseverance or his patience?

A young woman is sitting on the steps of a house. She is playing the guitar and singing. She has a lisp. Isn't she beautiful? You want to go to her and stay with her forever. Why isn't this possible? You have come so far.

A church has built a special box out near the sidewalk. It is full of free Bibles. The box says, "Take One." Next door, a man stands outside a used-book store. He has built a box too. It is full of old beat-up copies of *Walden.* His box says, "Take One," too. All of this hope in one block!

You pass a hardware, a drugstore, a café, a jeweler, a shoe shop, a dress outlet, a gas station. You sit at a bus stop and look around. You can see that the Decatur Road dead-ends at the courthouse just a block or two away. The world seems very old and all past. Up the street a bit a man in a second-story window wads up a piece of paper and tosses it out the window onto the sidewalk. You get up and walk to the spot. There are five or six balls of paper there. You pick up the one he just tossed out, smooth out the wrinkles and read it. He has written about you, walking down the street and sitting at the bus stop. The man is still at the window, sitting at an old desk. "Hey," you yell at him, "hey, you." He stands up and pokes his head out of the open window. "Save this," you say, and you hold out the crumpled page and smile. He smiles back. Lord, the things you are going to tell him!

57

And this was his prayer, his song:

"Haw, shump, Barney, shump." The old mule (Barney Number Five, great-great grandson, so to speak, of that old Father's mule) leaned deeper to the soil, yanking the man behind him, who for an instant fell to one knee and then only gradually stumbled back up to both feet. He wanted to curse but held it, breathed instead, "You old mule."

He went on plowing, plowing through an Indian summer and morning that was silk to the sunburned land, that was pewter to the touch, that made the earth roll up from the plowshare as if it were a can of biscuits popping; plowing his way slowly down the hillside stubblefield with the mule, back and forth, running up against a barbed-wire strand on one end, and on the other against an old dirt road. The field ran two hundred feet to a creek, and was at the most an acre and a half, but it was all day.

He was an old man, older than the mule five times
surely, out in that field lonely plowing. Out there coaxing
himself to go on as much as the mule, to finish this row,
then the next, not to think about the whole field all at
once, for fear that would tire him before the walking did.
But it was the morning still, and there was no dust yet, and
the air was cool, the mule fresh. He thought he might do
it.

He was lank in his age, tall but bent a little in the
middle, and wore clothes that hung on him as if he were
a length of wire stretched across the backyard: khaki cotton trousers and a long-sleeved shirt that he buttoned to
the wrists and collar, so that the sun wore a ring on his
neck and put gloves on his hands, so that whenever he
took his shirt off he seemed like some great white-banded
bird. His hair was short, gray-white, all one length, which
he oiled and combed straight back making his nose and
chin seem to jut farther out if possible, far enough to have
the bench of old-timers at Perry's Store say that if he had
another lifetime to live, the chin would touch the nose if
the nose didn't beat the chin to it. To this he would take
his teeth out of his pocket and put them in, and smile, and
chop, and then everyone in the store would bend in their
middles a little more, and roar. He was an old man, older
than the mule five times, surely, out in that field lonely
plowing.

"Haw, shump, mule, shump." And again the mule leaning deeper to the soil, just enough to let the man think he
pulled harder, and the old man knowing that, but thinking it was enough, any more and he himself could not hold
on. He fought with the handles, trying to set himself in the
routine, and began to sweat. For a moment he thought it
would be too much. And then suddenly, against the physical strain, like snapping through a root with the blade, his
mind passed to his youth.

"Well, Jenny, I want to tell you I had a fine time this evening, and, I mean I hope that maybe sometime you might want to go out with me again. Sometime. I mean I think you're a real pretty and smart girl." He was tall, a dusty scarecrow. The girl and he were sitting on a porch swing, and he was doing all of the talking, and he knew it, and so he gazed intently at the cap in his lap and picked at the button on top. And then something happened. He had been talking again, about his mule or something, and suddenly he realized that something had made him stop talking. She must have kissed him. He lifted his head slowly, and Jesus, she must have, because she was looking in her lap, and then she looked up, blinked at him and looked down again. Jeeesus. He could almost remember the kiss was like kissing the silk on a baby's head. He got up and walked to the other end of the porch and looked out over the fields—just to be able to stand it. Oh, man. Man. And there, then, remembering that he was a Man, and that he had been kissed by a Woman, he sort of wandered back to the swing, and sat down right next to her, and she looked up and blinked again, and so he kissed her this time, but still, real careful.

The old man blinked, and saw the mule straining his neck to blink back at him. They had stopped at the end of a furrow. He yelled, "Gee," and the mule blinked again and turned around for the next row. As the old man turned, he heard a horn beep. A small red truck had pulled up next to him on the side of the road. He could see a girl speaking to him, but could not hear her, and as he began to step over the ditch to get closer he thought of his teeth. They were out. He unbuttoned his shirt pocket, unwrapped the set from his handkerchief, and had almost thrown them in when he remembered her instructions to turn around when he did it in front of strangers. The young couple in the truck just looked at each other. He finally stepped across the ditch and turned his ear to the girl.

"Could you please tell us where the Barton farm auction is? It's supposed to be on this road, and we've been up and down it twice."

"Auction? Oh, yes, yes. You want the Barton place. Turn around and go back down the road about two miles more, and there'll be a little offshoot to the right, go with that. That'll lead you to the place."

And the girl, instead of asking again to make sure, or thanking him and going on, said, "Isn't it awfully hard work for you?"

And the old man, suddenly, uncomfortably, perceiving some inherent goodness in all women, said, "Yes, yes, it is," and said again, backing up, pointing, "About two miles more down this road and a little offshoot to the right; you won't miss it."

And as he turned, stepping back across the ditch, the truck shifted back into second gear, and the girl, after waving at his back, turned also, to look for the little offshoot on the Decatur Road.

"Haw, shump, Barney, shump." The mule shuddered to a start and the man allowed the share to slip gradually into the soil. He could count the passing of the day in the depth of his plowing. Up on high, the blade would drop to only ten inches and hit clay; as the hill sloped, the soil became deeper and finer, till at the bottom it plumbed to four feet. He and the mule sweated halfway down the hill, to fifteen inches and lunch. But the man not stopping there, plowing on, and the mule sensing this passing; at the end of each row he would lay his ears back and head for the tree he was usually fed under. Finally, the man raised his head from the ground passing underneath him, stopped the mule, and gazed toward the house. Then he remembered he had put his lunch under the tree with the mule's.

The mule broke for the tree when he felt the plow unhitched from his harness. The old man smiled, followed him, and poured the oats out on a piece of corrugated tin. As he leaned against the trunk of the tree and began to eat his own lunch, the cool wind blowing down the hollow began to dry his sweat. He shivered, and in the shivering fell again into his past.

The six of them passed through the door and into the house in one gulp, simultaneously slapping themselves, stomping their feet, each one claiming he was the closest to freezing to death. He carried an armful of firewood in, and after kicking each of his boys in the pants, he dropped the stack on the hearth and began to build a fire. He could feel Jenny standing behind him, blowing on her fingers, and so purposely took his time in splitting off the kindling and placing each stick in exactly the right position. When one sliver of wood fell off the kindling pile and he spent several minutes resetting it on the stack, she exploded. "Mitchell Parks, you good-for-nothing, you are purposely taking as long as possible to build that fire." And as she howled, she pulled him up from the hearth by the chin, and when he had risen, replaced him with a shove on the nose. "Now, I'll have that fire made this instant!"

The two burr-headed boys and the girls fell on the couch and hugged and slapped each other, laughing, until he, holding everything he had in, ordered them after more wood. When they'd gone, he stood up from the small flame and reached for Jenny, who pulled him toward her. As they fell apart from the embrace he reached into his coat pocket and pulled out a small snowball, dropping it into the front of her dress. She screamed around the room, wailing, cursing, and stopped only to beat on his shoulders when he caught her by the arms and whispered

188

in her ear, "Don't worry, Jenny, let me get it." She jerked on his nose, and breaking from his grasp, ran from the room. He stood there laughing on the hearth till he could laugh no more. And then, after standing there in the silence for a moment, after looking around the room once or twice, it tickled him again, and he laughed again, louder.

"Hey, you old codger, what out in the middle of all this field is so funny?" A short, heavy man with a John Deere cap on stepped down off his tractor. The old man turned over on his knees and pushed himself up from the ground with both hands; he recognized his neighbor and shook arms with him. "Why, you were just sitting there laughing as hard as I've seen a man laugh. What are you up to?"

The neighbor stood short and solid, all smile. The old man couldn't see any other way out of it than to say, "Well," kick the dirt, look up, turn around, again say, "Well," and just laugh some more.

"Well, don't tell me then. I just come over to see if I couldn't help out with some of this plowin'. Looks like you got most of it done. Why don't you let me take the tractor here and run up and down those last few rows, you know, might's well let that old mule have the rest of the day off. It won't take the tractor a tenth of the time it'd take him."

The old man kicked the dirt again. "No, no, Ben Webster, I reckon me and Barney can finish it up. I've got two grandsons comin' out in the morning. They're going to seed the winter rye for me; I figured they'd like that, but I guess I ought to finish up here."

The neighbor shifted his feet, rubbed his forearm and said, "Well, yeah, Mitch." The two men stood under the tree with their hands shoved in their pockets, looking out over the field at a group of swallows skimming the furrows, snatching bugs the plow had turned up. And then the neighbor said, "Well, got to be on my way then," and got back up on his tractor.

"Thanks anyway, Ben. I appreciate it."

"No problem." He drove off.

"Haw, shump, you Barney, pull." The old man leaned on the crossbar between the plow handles, holding the blade in the earth with his chest, keeping his eyes fixed on the furrow passing beneath him. With each step the mule shook its head up and out, chomping on the bit, but still pulling, still jerking the man after him. And then the old man fell. He fell and lay on the ground. The mule stopped, snorted in the dust. The man let his cheek rest against one side of the furrow, breathing out a small hollow in the soil. The ground smelled deep and heavy, and it was surprisingly warm this late in the fall, he thought. He lifted his head slowly; the furrow lay straight out before him, converging on the metal blade, and the mule stood above the whole earth. There was a swallow tottering on one of the plow handles. My, the ground was warm. Everything seemed so still now. He pushed himself up and sat on his haunches. The mule turned and looked back, pricking both ears up.

"C'mon, Barney, let's finish." They began again.

And again the man leaned on the crossbar, his hands grasping the worn handles, his elbows sticking out far behind his shoulders, over his back. And not even looking up when the mule stopped at the end of a row, but yelling, "Gee," and the mule turning on his own, while the old man kept pressure on the blade. He lost track soon, forgot the depth of the soil and forgot the sun, just listened to the swallows feeding. He turned up a rock and knew it from some other turning up while plowing forty years ago. And he finished. The mule stopped; he yelled, "Gee," but no movement. He walked himself

190

back up to standing with the aid of the handles, and looked over into the creek. "Good mule," and a pat on the flank.

The old man unhitched the plow and dropped the gear off the mule in the field. "Go on, git." The sun hung on the horizon like a cat hanging on the kitchen table, straining to see what was left of the dinner. "You go on, Barney, git to the shed." For a moment the old mule lingered in the half-light, then stepped slowly toward his stall. The man stooped to pick up the gear, and after three steps under the weight, dropped it again, and let it lie there. It was a shameful thing to do, he thought, and headed for the house. He pulled himself up on the front porch and sat in the swing there and after a few minutes reached over his knees to pull off his workboots. At the moment it seemed to him the whole day was worth that pleasure. And he thought that it hadn't been such a bad day; there would be no more plowing until the spring. He reckoned the Barton place to be sold by now. Ben would be back home eating dinner. "No, no," he said, as he rose and walked to the end of the porch, "it's been a fine fall day." And then he remembered he had thought of that day last fall only six or seven times this day. And as he stared into the sliver of sun remaining, he had the thought that it was the same sun he had plowed under sixty years ago, and that this ground before him was the same warm earth. But these were only fleeting thoughts. It confused him, for a moment, whether sixty years was a very short time, or a very long one. And as he stood there, watching the day pass on, watching the last few swallows skim the furrows and then bank up into the dusk, he thought he felt the first cold wind of early winter pass over him, and turning to the house, he fixed on the idea of getting out an extra quilt for the night ahead.

Selah.

58

You have been walking. There is a little park here in front of the Decatur courthouse. It is such a simple thing to say the leaves are all gone. You know that there are more decisions to be made. But it is so cold out. A nap would be nice. Just a short one. And maybe after you wake up, and have cleared the sleep from your eyes, you can add up all the things in the whole world you can count on, like the return of spring, and go from there. Go up the steps of the courthouse maybe, through the long hallway and out the back door, down the alley that joins, somewhat inconspicuously, Highway 69, which goes all the way to the Pacific. Or maybe, as you wrap your coat around you and lean up against an old oak, maybe, you decide, you can just turn around, like the tide and the blood and the ancient dusk, and go back home.